ABE AND LUCINDA

The Curse

Eugenia Springer

ESproductions

A Folktale
The characters and events portrayed in this book are fictitious. Any similarity to real persons, living or dead, is coincidental and not intended by the author.

ISBN-13: 9798679170735

Cover design by: the author
Printed in the United States of America
Contact:journeybooks43@gmail.com

Dedicated
to all
Who are Caribbean children at heart
and
to
The Memory of
Dr. Roy Bryce-LaPorte (1933 to 2012)
A Sociologist, Dr. Bryce-LaPorte was a Scholar of the African Diaspora and Black Migration to and from The United States; and the founding director in 1973 of the Research Institute On Immigration and Ethnic Studies at The Smithsonian Institution

"... And your memory of this night

Will be gone by morning light

You will wander far and wide

'Till scalded and despised

You return here to this place

Seeking out her face.

If she still

Your love would be

Then from this curse

You would be free".

EXCERPTED FROM THE FOLKTALE, "ABE & LUCINDA"
BY EUGENIA SPRINGER

CONTENTS

A SCARED WIDOW

Long, long ago, deep inside a quiet forested village on a small tropical island, there lived a very scared widow and her four young sons. Young Ma Beatrice and her sons had fled to an old house at the end of a winding north to south road called Cemetery Road.

Just a few years earlier, it seemed, the young mother had been the happy daughter of Pa Alfred Worrell and Ma Elmina Worrell. The old house at the edge of the vast forest had been her childhood home. That was where Warren had proposed to her.

She was eighteen years old when Warren Bartelay visited the village of Tapara. The young admirer had traveled from a neighboring village about fifteen miles away to meet the parents of this girl he had met while taking Commercial lessons in the city.

Although the twenty-two-year-old was not particularly handsome, he had an honest face. This immediately won over the hearts of Beatrice's parents. Unknown to Beatrice, Warren, had just one reason for asking for her address that day at school. He wanted to meet her father and mother.

On his first meeting with Pa and Ma Worrell, to Beatrice's

shocking surprise, Warren confessed his love for their daughter, and asked their permission to marry the eighteen-year-old.

Not only was Beatrice the beloved daughter of Pa Alfred Worrell and Ma Elmina Worrell, she was also a beloved daughter of the village of Tapara. The entire village therefore received news of the proposal with great joy.

Every family in the neighborhood was invited to the wedding, and when the time came Taparans joyously opened their doors to Warren's people.

Apart from his parents, grandparents, aunts, uncles, cousins, and friends, Warren was accompanied by a look-alike from his village, his twin brother, Waldo.

In the midst of their week-end long celebrations the people had fun mistaking one twin for the other.

But things had changed. So, until she could find a better way to keep her children safe, Beatrice would make the old isolated house with its sweet memories, her home.

ABE LOVES LUCINDA

His chest felt so tight, he didn't know what to do. Another day of heavy sadness for this well beloved youth in the small town of Gleam.

Hardly beyond boyhood, the young man inhaled deeply, then let out the air forcefully. Another deep breath, another forceful expulsion of air.

Just when he had been counting the days to his proposal —to that time when he could approach Lucinda's parents and ask for the lovely girl's hand in marriage—an interfering foreign woman showed up in their little hometown.

It did not matter to him that the woman had been telling whoever would listen that she was determined to be his wife. He did not care about the attractive older woman. All he wanted was to tell the teenager he loved so passionately that waiting for her parents' permission to marry her was hard.

Patience, Abe, he told himself. Just six more months to her graduation.

Rules were rules. He could not ask for her hand in marriage before she graduated—not if he wanted to be in her parents' good graces. He knew that; she knew that; and her parents expected nothing less. He must do nothing to interfere with her educational development.

Even before his elderly adoptive parents had died, when he was seventeen, he had two goals he wanted to accomplish before his twenty-fifth birthday. One, he wanted to be an accountant, and two, he wanted to get Mister Holder's permission to marry his lovely daughter, Lucinda.

At age twenty-two, he had been an accountant for a couple years. And in a few months he would propose to Lucinda.

Plans were falling in place. He had already identified the ring in the jewelry shop in Gleam, their village town. And he had the full payment in an envelope, labelled, 'Lucinda's engagement ring'. The envelope was in the bottom drawer of his nine-foot tall polished mahogany wardrobe.

Several parents in and around Gleam wished the gentlemanly, ambitious Abe would be their son-in-law. Also, a few mothers in their church community wished Lucinda would see in their son more than just a 'nice brother'.

But none of that mattered. Everybody in the quaint town of Gleam knew that Abe loved Lucinda and the chatty, bubbly lovely teenager had eyes for no one but Abe.

All that was until Madam Veroux settled in Gleam, and all by herself saw a future husband in the good-looking, progressive-thinking younger man, called Abe Chavier.

◆◆◆

The newcomer had not kept it a secret that she had arrived in Gleam in search of a husband. Age did not matter much as long as the man was not much older than she. Even before Abe was aware of her presence in the quiet little town, she had spotted the unassuming but handsome youth among the townspeople and had settled it in her mind that he was the man for her.

For the preceding eighteen months, Lucinda had been his motivation to rise up early on mornings and serenade another new day. Although a brisk walk would take him just about ten minutes to get from his neighborhood to her parents' home, seeing her whenever he wanted to was not an option.

Neighbors back there, in the sparsely populated bushy neighborhood where Abe grew up, would smile as they listened to him every morning singing, "Goodnight Irene, goodnight my love, I'll meet you in my dreams".

But the melodious voice had the boys' plan

been silenced, it seemed.

On the other side of town, Lucinda was waking up on mornings with a sharp pain in her heart. She did not know why Abe no longer dropped in, at least once a week, when he rode his bike along her street.

She refused to believe the buzzing rumor that he had fallen for another woman, much less, someone about twice his age.

The love of her heart had never directly told her that he loved her. Although he had spoken to mutual friends about his love for her. But actions speak louder than words, so Lucinda knew the young church treasurer was hers, and she was his.

The church community knew this, and their neighbors knew this.

Her parents knew this also, and Abe himself could not have shown more commitment to her if they had been engaged.

It used to be that at least once a week he would slow his bike to a halt as he rode along their street, and drop in for a short chat with her parents. But he really longed to just see her.

During that fifteen or twenty minutes, she would emerge from inside the house, and show her face for about five minutes. Ron Holder did not miss the way Abe kept his eyes on Lucinda during her short visit to the gallery. Nor did he miss the young man's patient sigh whenever Lucinda excused herself and went back inside the house.

There was no doubt in Ron Holder's mind that Abe was in love with his daughter. The boy had not yet turned eighteen when he had confided to the older man that one day he, Ron Holder, would be his father-in-law. Abe's elderly adoptive parents had both passed on, and to the concern of his deceased parents' friends, Abe had opted for living alone till he married the girl of his dream. But he never breathed a word of his intention to Lucinda.

Every Sunday, after he had attended to the church

collections, like a man deeply in love, Abe would stand in the doorway, scanning the small crowd in the country churchyard.

Everybody would know he was looking for the bubbly, chatty Lucinda.

They were both youth leaders and had lots of time during church activities and church sponsored activities to be around each other, but that time on Sundays was their alone time. They would chat for about half an hour without any member interrupting them.

That would be the only time in any week that he would spend quality time, one on one with her.

Unaware of his promise to her father, Lucinda, often wondered how much Abe cared for her. She loved him so much! Did he care for her enough to want to marry her, she often wondered?

There were other lovely girls in the church community. He talked with everyone. And everyone liked him.

His eagerness to be in her company and his consistency in making time every Sunday to talk with just her, she took as evidence that he was devoted to her and her alone.

SORCERESS WANTS ABE

He was missing her, but he had to do what he had to do. And aware that he was leaving plenty room for misunderstanding, he had to risk throwing even her mind into confusion if that was what it took to protect her.

Now, no more of his heart pounding, willing her to come out into the gallery and spend more than her usual five minutes as he visited with her parents in their verandah. No more gazing into her gentle eyes for those brief five minutes she would show her face before excusing herself and hurrying back into the house.

In painful reminiscence, he smiled wryly at how Lucinda would quickly look away when his eyes locked onto hers—whenever *their eyes made four*.

It was okay for him to occasionally drop in to visit her family for a few minutes. But he could not drop by to just visit with her. He had to get her parents' permission to do that.

He knew what was expected. He had to write a letter to Mister Holder asking permission to marry his daughter. That would be the proposal letter. Lucinda's parents would accept his proposal if they trusted him to treat their daughter honorably, and to take care of her financially.

Once his proposal was accepted he would be allowed to visit Lucinda. And her parents would take her to visit his home. Then together, they all would plan for the engagement, and after that, the wedding.

His life was working according to plans until that interfering woman settled in Gleam and gave the impression that she had some hold on him.

Truly he had been so happy, knowing that beautiful Lucinda had eyes only for him despite the interest some of his friends at church had in her.

Considering what was going on with him, he could not blame her for keeping her eyes averted from him when they attended church.

How could he expect her to understand that it was out of love for her that he had stopped dropping by her home at least once a week; that he had stopped spending time with her in the church yard after service every Sunday. How would any reasonable girl understand his convoluted thinking!

Now, during church services, he could only painfully gaze on the girl he loved, and wince as he felt her deep sadness. He understood why she avoided his gaze even when she knew he was looking at her. But it was better this way.

Never in his life had he felt so helpless, so painfully helpless. He was no weakling; no coward. He would defend

Lucinda with his life. But what he had found out about the woman in gaudy head wraps and colorful, flouncy skirts, melted his courage.

Whisperings in the town had reached his ears. The woman behaving as though she had some hold on him was a sorceress!

The thought of an obeah woman keeping her eyes on him was terrifying. He was petrified for himself but moreso for Lucinda.

There was no threat he would back away from to protect his beloved! Even at risk of losing his life! But sorcery? How could he fight that? How had his life come to this?

If he confided his dilemma to Lucinda and her parents, they might try to help him. This could put them in the woman's plain sight. He couldn't take that risk.

How could he promise Mister Holder to protect his daughter if he couldn't even protect himself?

LUCINDA CONFUSED

Unknown to Lucinda, he had given her father a key to his house. Just in case. Both his elderly adoptive parents had died of natural causes.

Some family friends like Ron Holder and his wife, had always looked out for him since then.

With a clean rag, he thoughtfully wiped the inside of the lamp shade.

For the second time that night, he carried his silver long-barrel torchlight into the narrow hallway and carefully checked the padlock on the backdoor. It was locked.

After turning down the wick of the kerosene lamp, with a soft weary sigh, he slowly pulled the coverlet over his body, up to his neck. Thankful for heavy doors and windows toning down the cacophony of nocturnal whistling and groaning frogs, Abe welcomed the darkness as he shut his eyes. Silently he cried out, praying that the morrow would provide a way out of his dilemma.

In the midst of the muffled night sounds, a cock crowed. On impulse Abe got up and pressed his knees onto the hard floor.

"Father in heaven", he wept, "have mercy on me. Lord God, protect Lucinda and her parents. Please Lord God, protect them from this woman. O God, I am petrified. Jesus Lord, I don't know what to do. I am frightened. I am terrified. O Father, I don't know what to do. Please, watch over me, Lord Jesus! Please. Please! O God, please! Amen".

Pulling himself together, he got back under his coverlet. Mercifully, a deep sleep calmed his mind.

His future wife and her parents were troubled. They just could not understand why he had stopped dropping by the house, and why he had stopped lingering in the church yard after church on Sundays.

He had longed to let the sweet almost-eighteen-year-old know that night and day, his thoughts were only of her. He had prayed that she would trust him, and know how anxious he was for her to pass her exams and graduate so they could get on with their plans to be man and wife.

He had not told her that he had already put away money for her engagement ring and that in his wardrobe he had a draughtsman's plan for the renovation of the two-bedroom house his parents had left him. He should include her in the planning, but he could not *put the cart before the horse;* he first had to talk to her parents.

How could such beautiful prospects suddenly fade into just wishful thinking! Lucinda was questioning whether or not he really wanted a future with her. This much was hinted in the occasional comments dropped by a member, or friend, in passing.

Now, greater than his desire to make Lucinda his wife, was his obsession about keeping her and her parents away from the woman.

No one the young man knew could say where this woman had come from, or who she was. People were apprehensive about her. And many were intrigued by her bold shameless play for the younger man's attention.

Now, he could no longer venture out into the small town without feeling jittery. Wherever he was in the town of Gleam, he would glance around and find the woman next to him, or not far away.

With shopping list and basket in hand, he had been in the shop, among townspeople chit-chatting while waiting his turn at the counter. Outside, the air was cool, and in the coming and going of shoppers, the atmosphere in the well-stocked enclosed marketplace felt buoyant and friendly.

At one end of the long counter, the shopkeeper was filling out Mister Gibbs' order. Everyone knew that the reserved Bajan gentleman always shopped for his young wife, Betty. Unlike Abe, Mister Gibbs did not own a bike, and had no transportation, so rather than have his young wife walk the three quarter mile distance from the shop to their home, toting a heavy basket, the older gentleman did the shopping.

Patiently, Abe was waiting his turn.

Just outside the shop, his bike was one of three leaning against the outer wall. Once his order was filled, he would strap his basket onto the saddle of his bike and ride home with hands unencumbered.

The line behind him was growing, but just two persons were ahead of him. Waiting, without getting in line, Deacon Onello and his wife, Sister Elmeena, were standing across from him. He returned their friendly smile, as they waited their turn.

Unaware that anyone had crept up close behind him, he was shocked and startled by the woman's voice almost in his ear.

"Abe Chavier, handsome and intelligent young man, I am several years older than you, but look at me. I am youthful looking, and I have great wealth, and great power. We can be a powerful team in this country—you and I . . ."

He did not look at her. Instead, suppressing disgust and agitation, he calmly glanced to his right, at Deacon Onello, and his very talkative wife, Sister Elmeena.

Huddling close to them were Miss Edith and Miss Irene, two older spinsters, who as they liked to say, knew him before he was born.

Everybody in the shop had been life-long residents of Gleam. Everyone except this disgusting woman intruding in his space right behind him.

Silence fell in the shop. The young man felt ambushed.

Was that a look of condemnation he had briefly glimpsed coming from Sister Elmeena?

Lucinda had turned down the Onello's son, Oba, when he had asked her to be his girlfriend. It was common knowledge in the small Christian church community that Sister Elmeena Onello was restrained in her dealings with the young church treasurer, Abe Chavier.

Taking a quick visual sweep of the space around him, Abe glimpsed familiar faces smothered in embarrassment.

". . . I can give you everything you want . . . everything you have ever desired for yourself", the woman continued shamelessly.

The warm breath on his neck stoked his repulsion.

". . . And I will be a great wife."

In his peripheral vision, Sister Elmeena's stare hardened. Involuntarily, his fists clenched.

". . . Will you marry me?"

Slowly, Abe stepped away from the woman. Then he turned around, and without blinking, looked hard into the flirtatious eyes of the smiling woman, and in a flat disinterested tone, for the first time, addressed the woman. "No, Ma'am", he spoke respectfully. "You are old enough to be my mother; I can never marry you."

Like one stung, the madam jumped back, screeching, "You will regret ever saying that to me!"

And lifting her elegantly wrapped head, and tilting her proud chin upward, the fiftyish year old woman strutted to the open door.

Less than half an hour later, as he stepped out on the roadside, pushing his bike, his friend, Trevor, hailed out to him. "Boy", Trevor walked up close to Abe, "you in anything with that woman? You have Lucinda in pain".

"Trevor, things are not always as they seem. I just talked to that woman for the first time. It wasn't nice. Lucinda is the only person I will ever love . . ."

"Boy, what happen? Look how your hands shaking! Good Lord, Abe, what happen? You look like you've seen a ghost!"

"I feel terrified. But only God can help me. I have to be careful. The woman . . . is a witch. An obeah woman."

"An obeah woman, boy? You sure?"

"That's what I heard. I have to keep Lucinda and her family safe. Tell Lucinda that everything I have been doing has been about keeping her safe. I would rather die than cause Lucinda to suffer. I would never love anybody but Lucinda. The woman seems to be keeping her eyes on me. That is why I stay away from Lucinda and her family."

"Obeah, boy? This woman who the whole town is saying, is always on your heels, is an obeah woman? Boy, be careful."

"You keep yourself safe too, Trevor."

"So how you would get out of this pickle, boy?"

"I don't know. You better go your way. I won't want her targeting you too."

The well-populated town was a lively community. Before Trevor could get to Lucinda, Sister Elmeena had visited the home of Brother and Sister Holder. Seeing an opportunity to shift Lucinda's interest to her son, Oba, a lovely young man, Sister Elmeena gave an altered version of what she witnessed in the shop.

At church, Rita Holder avoided his eyes. She marveled at how wrong they had been. Abe had changed from the boy she thought she always knew. She never expected him to cause her daughter so much pain.

But Ron Holder, Lucinda's father, felt there was something they were missing. Abe's behavior was not normal. He was not behaving like a man who had fallen out of love with Lucinda.

He was more like a lover in anguish. Besides, Ron had known Elmeena all his life and refused to allow her twisted mind and poison tongue to destroy his confidence in Abe.

The older man wished Abe would trust him enough to confide in him about whatever the problem was. But instead of seeking counsel among his elders at church, every Sunday, the obviously troubled young man would now jump on his bike as soon as he was through counting and recording the church offering, and under the sad gaze of Lucinda and other perplexed members, would pedal away.

LUCINDA'S PREMONITION

The suffering girl's midnight scream jolted her parents and sent them scrambling into her room!

"Papa! Papa! Oh God, help! Help!"

Doubled over, and clutching her stomach, the rocking teenager moaned, "Abe! Abe! God, protect Abe! Please Father, protect Abe!"

Embracing her daughter, the distraught Mom pleaded, "A bad dream, Lucinda?" But the girl just rocked and moaned, "Papa, Abe needs help! Abe needs help! Please! O God, have mercy, have mercy! Abe!" And screaming, the girl burst into hysterical sobs.

"Tell us what's happening with you, my daughter. What about Abe?"

"He is in danger, Papa. I just know it. Something terrible is happening. I am feeling it. Please, Papa, please! Abe! Please, please Papa. Oh God, please."

ABE IN TROUBLE

Struggling to conceive of a way, any way, to bypass the woman's interference . . . to escape her focus . . . to become irrelevant to her so he could continue to safely interact with Lucinda, he got out of bed and sat at the little table.

How could his beautiful life suddenly go so wrong? Weekends held so much promise. On Saturdays while riding his bike along her street, he would pull into her yard and spend fifteen to twenty minutes chatting with her parents even as he telepathically willed her to come out to the verandah and be more generous with her time as she lingered briefly in his company. Then Sunday.

Everybody dressed their best and looked their smartest for church. There was no rush. The Lord's Day was the one day of the week when they were free to leisurely spend time in each other's company. In the sanctuary they would position themselves so they could discretely observe each other throughout the service. At least once a month he would accept the Holder's invitation to Sunday lunch. Later on, after lunch, as involved youth leaders they would have lots of opportunities to mix and mingle with other youth.

They were in love! That was the one open secret in that little Christian church community! Abe and Lucinda were in love with each other!

Seeing Lucinda on the weekend, chatting with her, jointly participating in youth meetings, was the secret promise Friday nights held.

What would a fifty something-year-old woman want with a church going youth? And of all the men, old and young, in the sleepy little town of Gleam, why would she want to latch onto him?

Stalked? That was now his reality? He was being stalked?

Spending a relaxing evening on the football field and hanging out afterwards with the players was no longer a favorite Friday evening pastime. Hours earlier he had been way back there near the goalpost, leaning up on his bike, when on impulse he glanced back. And there she was. Immediately he had jumped on his bike and rode off.

Two days earlier, as he was having his hair cut, at the junction in Gleam, Mister Mitchell, the kind elderly barber, had mumbled in his ear, "Son, stay cool, but the madam is standing across the road, looking in here. Be careful".

It was weird how the woman kept turning up wherever he was. She didn't seem to care who was around or who was hearing her whenever she boldly spoke of her love for him. Dreading the pain reports getting back to Lucinda would cause the young love of his life, he could only wince.

Confused about how to shake off the nuisance of a woman, he was determined about one thing—he would stay away from Lucinda and her family just to lessen chances of the woman identifying them as a problem.

Since he never knew when the woman was watching, now whenever he rode along Lucinda's street, he kept his gaze straight ahead, and maintained his regular speed as his bike approached her house.

Hating the tension, the unwelcomed intrusion in his life was generating between himself and the girl he loved, night and day he wrangled with the problem--how to free himself from the unwelcomed attention.

In the dim light of the kerosene lamp, the young man stood up, stepped out to the narrow hallway and checked the back door. And as he did every night, he placed the padlock on the latch and locked it; then he again stretched out supine on his bed, thinking.

He had knelt beside his bed when concern for the pain Lucinda was enduring pushed him to his knees. Now he was back under his light coverlet.

Petrified and dumbfounded, as he watched the woman, in the diffused light, standing beside his double bed, he desperately questioned himself—did I lock that door, or did I just think of locking it but forgot? How could this woman get into my locked room!

“Oh God, deliver me!” he silently screamed as panic battered his will to survive the drag of his body into a sea of billowing darkness.

“You fool . . ." the words smashed through his crumbling bastion of courage. "Nobody rejects me and gets to boast about it! Till the day I die You will eat like a dog and at night sleep in a sty. And your memory of this night will be gone by morning light. You will wander far and wide till scalded and despised, you return here to this place seeking out her face; if she still your love would be, then from my curse you will be free”.

“Sit up!” Mockingly the flickering idea swept past his mind. Then in a daze he struggled with the thought—*this must be death.*

And Abe Chavier was no more. That night he disappeared.

PA WORRELL'S FAMILY

Although the outlying areas of Tapara were sparsely populated, around the center of the village, houses were built close to one another. This was so on Cyril Hill, and around the bend, north of the hill.

Before she had fled to her old family house at the southern end of the long winding pitch path known as Cemetery Road, Ma Beatrice had lived in one of the houses on the hill.

Pa Alfred Worrell and Ma Alfred within a few years had become the proud grandparents of first, Calvin, then Joshua, and then Canaan, and Elijah. For a few years Warren and his wife had kept Ma Cyril, the local midwife, busy.

But even before Calvin was born Warren had built his house in the expansive yard at the top of the hill, two house lots above the blue lepayed house that for many years had been the home of Pa Cyril Fred and Ma Cyril.

Beatrice was approaching her sixteenth birthday when her parents had made the long trip to the city to secure a ninety-nine-year lease of the two house lots for their daughter.

Small family homes dotted both sides of the massive slope.

Every neighbor's house on the hill was within a ten second walk from their next door neighbor's. And every household had a kitchen garden back of their house.

Anyone could stand up there back of the houses on the eastern side of the hill and see Cemetery Road running down below along the foot of the hill, and then spooling off southward, like a long ribbon. Beyond the road, to the east, was bush, as far as the eye could see. And beyond the bush, in different directions were several sparsely populated neighborhoods, some separated by miles, but all in the village of Tapara.

Even as the neighborhood *gayippe* was constructing Warren's house, Pa Fred had called together Pa Manny, his next door neighbor, and Warren, and laid out the case that the Cyril Hill neighborhood and surrounding populated areas had collectively become a growing community. The men agreed. Pa Fred then suggested that Warren establish a shop right there on the hill to serve the entire community of Tapara.

Pa Manny Clarke, whose thatched-roof two-bedroom house was located between Pa Fred's home of many years, and Warren's new house, liked the idea. His twenty-three-year-old son, Robert, an apprentice in masonry and carpentry, would help.

Warren and Beatrice had *put their heads together* to come up with a lay-out plan for the shop. Once there was a blue-print for the builders to follow, Pa Worrell had called back together the team of men who had built Warren's house, to construct the shop.

Using well cured mora and mahogany logs that had been felled under the right moon, the gayippe erected a sturdy fourteen by fourteen-foot wooden structure complete with a galvanize shed-roof, towering nine feet above the six-foot wide doorway.

From inside the shop, wide double doors opened onto the sturdy mahogany step. The rugged out-door step consisting of two eight by three-foot treads, and supported by six-inch high risers, was built to last.

Customers coming up the slope would comfortably mount the steps to enter through the heavy double doors. Once in the shop, they would have a five-foot wide floor space in front the wide counter.

Before the workers had even constructed the wide counter, and the shelves on the wall, they had sectioned off a six by four-foot-wide area on the western side of the room. A narrow doorway led from this room to the outside yard.

The two-room structure was a three-second step down from Warren's wire-netting enclosed yard.

From sunrise to sunset, the builders had worked non-stop.

While they dug holes to plant posts, and sawed boards to put up walls and lay down flooring, the women had cooked breakfast, lunch, and dinner, for the team. Running on the camaraderie generated by team work, workers had pushed on way into the night and completed their project in less than one month.

That was how it came to be that Warren and his wife, Beatrice, owned the shop up there on Cyril Hill in the Cemetery Road neighborhood.

THE WORRELL'S DAUGHTER

Canaan was a young baby when his grandfather, Pa Alfred Worrell, died. Crunched in sadness, the neighborhood came together in a wake to celebrate Pa Worrell's life, even as the men built his coffin.

With heavy hearts and lots of weeping Pa Alfred Worrell was covered in the grave dug by hands he had helped guide into adulthood.

About one year after the revered elder of Tapara had been buried, his faithful, loving, but grieving wife also quietly went to her rest.

Beatrice felt devastated. The little ones shed lots of tears. After their grandpa's passing, they had come to a clearer understanding of death as goodbye forever.

Again, the men from the community built a coffin, and lovingly lowered their beloved village mother in the hole dug next to the man whom she had loved all her life, and with whom she had joyously aged.

Beatrice and her husband, her boys, and neighbors, were sad for a long time. The village grieved for Pa Worrell and for his wife. Neighbors wondered how Beatrice would cope with losing both parents within the space of one year. They were glad that the young mother had found in Warren, a loving husband who cherished her.

Meanwhile, in Gleam, despite the passing of years, the people were still in an uneasy state over the sudden, strange disappearance of Abe. No one spoke of him as though he had been long gone. And certainly none spoke as though he would never return.

Lucinda had accepted the police report that Abe was a missing person. There was no reason to suspect that he had died, they had said. Maybe he just wanted to leave town and not be found, they suggested.

Although to onlookers, she appeared resigned to her loss, inwardly Lucinda was anguished. Considering what she had heard from Trevor, and the talk sweeping through the town, even talk within her church, about the woman having stalked Abe, she was convinced that something unnatural had befallen her Love.

But she wasn't giving up hope. If he was alive, and she believed with all her heart, that despite what might have happened, he was still breathing, she would find him.

Prayer was the only way to dissolve evil effects.

Through her initiatives, prayer groups sprung up

throughout the church island-wide membership as members refused to give in to the 'doer of evil' as the sorceress was labelled. There was a steely determination in some groups to prove that good trumps evil, that when one or two become infused with the power of God, evil effects cease to exist.

Since her horrific screams had sent neighbors scampering through the bush to Abe's house in the wee hours of that Saturday morning, she had started the practice of not just praying for, but claiming protection and restoration of, Abe.

For the first month, accompanied by her parents, she visited Abe's house every day. For hours at a time while her parents cleared weed from around his house, and cobwebbed the place, she would curl up on his bed and bawl. Attending classes was out of the question. Schoolbooks no longer interested her.

What had happened to Abe? She had to figure this out in order to find him.

And she did not want to live if she could not find him.

There was nothing ordinary about his disappearance. His bike was still in its place in the narrow corridor. His toothbrush hung in the wooden toothbrush rack nailed on the wall above the basin stand. His bed had looked like he was just lying in it. Even his alpagatas were beside his bed on the crocus bag mat with woven colored scraps of cloth.

Trevor had told her about the witch. Mister Mitch, the barber, had told her father about the stalker. Even some of the young footballers had shared their concern with her family about the woman stalking Abe.

Could Abe be trying to escape the woman all this time, she wondered. Or did she somehow have him trapped somewhere?

She couldn't go there. She couldn't allow herself to even conceive of him being overpowered and under demonic control.

After several weeks of hair-pulling grief, overnight, it seemed, Lucinda's parents witnessed a dramatic change in their daughter. The teenager had pulled herself together, and ordered her living as a matured woman with a purpose.

While she grieved, her parents had feared she might miss out on graduating with her class, but she had picked herself up, returned to school, and graduated with the highest honors.

Something in her attitude had also changed. Her chattiness gave way to seriousness, and her bubbly demeanor yielded to an obviously introspective approach to everything, every situation.

Lucinda had changed. With a no-nonsense attitude, she promptly dismissed every eligible young man who tried to replace Abe in her heart. Much to Oba's disappointment. Despite the passing of many years, in her soul, she knew Abe would return some day. Till then she would be true to him.

Faithfully she attended to the upkeep of his house. No repair was ever needed, because no part of the structure was allowed to deteriorate. No furniture or appliance needed repair because every item in the house was maintained in top shape.

WIDOWED, BEATRICE WEDS

Married women in the village were called Madam, or Ma, as a sign of respect. The Ma or Madam was followed by the first name of their husband, so the young woman, Beatrice, after marriage, was called Madam Warren.

Warren Bartelay was a very kind husband, a playful, loving father, and a thoughtful provider. He was also an excellent carpenter. When Madam Warren was pregnant with Canaan, her husband realized his family needed more room at the dining table, so he put his skills to work.

Calvin and Joshua enjoyed hanging around the workbench every evening after the shop was closed. They stood around and watched their Papa saw, chisel, and shave the board and wood. They were fascinated when they saw him stain and polish their new table which looked like it was bought in a joiner's shop.

A larger table necessitated a larger tablecloth, so Beatrice ripped and bleached extra flour bags to join together to make the larger tablecloth. She enjoyed spreading the new starched and ironed embroidered white table cloth on the table at mealtime.

Warren's place was at the head of the table. She sat to his

right. Calvin liked to sit between both parents. He would pull up a chair at the corner of the table. Joshua usually pulled up his chair on the other side of his Papa. Canaan was satisfied as long as he was fed by his Mama.

Mealtime was fun at the Bartelay family home. Warren led the family in pleasant chit chats. And he casually taught his boys to say, “Grace before meals” and “Grace after meals”. Even toddler Canaan could say “Grace before meals” and “Grace after meals” by heart.

A particular father, Warren taught his boys what he called, good table manners.

As much as possible they were to avoid belching, or belching loudly, and when chewing food, their mouth should be closed.

With lots of giggling, young Calvin and Joshua listened attentively. They looked really tickled when their Papa said to them, “No one would like food pellets from their mouth ending up on another person’s plate, or worse yet, on another person’s face. Chewing food and talking don’t go together; it even looks impolite”.

Years later when they were bigger boys, Calvin and Joshua felt glad that they had been living by the rules their Papa had taught them.

Warren lovingly guided his boys. He showed so much interest in teaching them even little ways of being polite, and industrious. It was as though he wanted them to learn everything they could, from him.

About moving chairs, he taught them to lift, not drag. And he was not rushing them. No. He just casually shared with them whatever he thought would be helpful to them.

The caring father even had the boys memorize a list of what he called, 'nice feeling' words.

"Excuse me, Thank you, Sorry, and Please, were words that made everybody feel good."

These words, give people a nice feeling, he said. "Before you leave the table", he lovingly told his young sons, "or before you leave anybody's presence, you should say, 'excuse me'."

And of course, he spoke about washing hands before meals. Before they sat at the table, as a custom, they held their hands over the basin while their Mama poured water from the jug.

Warren told his boys that these 'basic rules' would make dining in their company a pleasant experience.

Their Mama agreed with their Papa that if the boys practiced good table manners, anyone would enjoy dining in their company.

In addition to teaching the boys basic table manners, Warren joined his wife in teaching them what he called, personal hygiene. They taught the boys to wash behind their ears, and cleanse their nostrils, to brush their teeth, comb their hair, and keep their fingernails clean.

Once the boys had learned to take care of themselves,

Warren encouraged his wife to trust them to take care of their own personal hygiene.

When Beatrice said she enjoyed taking care of her sons' hygienic needs, even though she knew they were capable of taking care of themselves, Warren told her that a parent's work is lighter when children are taught to take care of themselves. Besides, he said, the children feel more self-confident when they know they can take care of themselves without having to be told.

In time, both parents proudly observed Calvin and Joshua, and at times, even little Canaan, with no prompting, washing their bodies, and in general, taking care of their personal hygiene. The boys grew up knowing that before dinner they bathed off, and after dinner they had to brush their teeth and change into their pajamas. By then their Mama would have scratched a match to light the wicks in the kerosene lamps.

The best part of their evening was after dinner. As it got dark outside they would sit in their living room, and listen to their Papa tell stories.

After bedtime story time, the family would kneel and say the "Our Father" Prayer, then with hugs and kisses from Papa and Mama, the young boys would slip into bed.

Warren was everything Beatrice wished for in a husband. Every day she felt she loved him more and more. But Mr. Warren Bartelay became ill, very ill. Elijah was just about one-year-old when his Papa had to be hospitalized.

Because children were not allowed in the hospital, Warren could not see his sons. The boys felt very sad. They wanted their Papa back home. Beatrice was very sad. She was missing her beloved husband around the house.

Tuberculosis was a dreaded disease. It was caused by a very dangerous germ. The entire village felt very apprehensive because everybody knew that people with TB hardly ever recovered.

Two years after his last child, Elijah, was born, Warren Bartelay, beloved husband of Beatrice Bartelay, died.

Tuberculosis took away Madam Warren's loving husband and left her alone with four young sons. The young widow was inconsolable.

About four years after her husband's death, the thirty-one-year-old mother allowed herself to arrange a marriage with a man who agreed to help with the shop. She, all on her own, convinced herself that the man would be a kind father to her boys.

Beatrice did not know what to make of the man. He was obviously homeless; answered in monosyllables; and never initiated a conversation.

Even when he responded to her he never looked at her; rather, his eyes would be focused on any space or object next to her. She thought he was going through hard times, and was just embarrassed. Yet the man was so helpful. That could only mean, she thought, that he cared.

In time he might become more self-confident, Beatrice said to herself, and prove to be just what she needed in a husband.

Every day he helped her pack groceries on the shelves, and fill out orders on customers' lists. When she looked at the Financial Records notebook he had written in, she could tell exactly how much stock she had left, or how much she needed to order from the delivery van.

Obviously, the man was a very talented and competent book-keeper. She marveled at the expert way he attended to every detail in the shop.

She was never out of stock and never short on change.

Her new assistant closed the shop promptly at five thirty every evening and every morning opened it on time. Thankful for the help, she was able to spend more time taking care of her children. It was almost like having Warren back.

As she observed the man closely she noticed that although he seemed to be homeless, he never took anything from the shop for himself, and he never asked any favors.

She interpreted his observed commitment to turning up every day, and his attention to details as indications that he cared for her and her children.

Just one thing bothered the widowed mother—the man did not interact with her sons. But this, she thought, was because he was embarrassed.

There was no doubt in her mind that if the man wasn't so shy he would propose. The more time she spent around him the more she was convinced they would make a great team—not that he showed the slightest interest in her.

Anyhow, Beatrice proposed. He could manage the shop, and in exchange he would share her home. That privilege came with three meals a day.

How could he turn down such a good offer, even though they had not known each other for any length of time?

She owed it to Warren to make sure his sons were brought up by somebody who was competent, as the man seemed to be. It didn't bother her that the man never even acknowledged her proposal. She understood him. He would do what she asked of him.

Villagers who had been spotting the man around the village felt sorry for Madam Warren. There was not one person in Tapara who could have vouched that the man helping Beatrice in the shop would be a caring person. But at the same time there also was not one person who could offer any reason why Beatrice should not try to make a civilized husband out of the unkempt, unshaven, evidently homeless man.

Because the young widow had been so heartbroken for so long, no one had the courage to caution her that Mister Harry might not be all she was hoping he would be.

UNDESIRABLE HUSBAND

It didn't take long for Beatrice to realize that marrying the weird man was a big mistake. The Cemetery Road neighborhood had about twenty to twenty-two homes—some made from tapia, and some from wood--along the two miles stretch between the shop and Ma Beatrice's home.

Vacant, bushy lots of land, called 'bandons, separated most of these houses.

Roughly midway along this distance, on the western side, was the village cemetery. Every Saturday and Sunday Beatrice and her boys spent time lovingly pulling weeds and decorating their three graves with freshly cut wild flowers. This way mother and sons kept their memory of Pa and Ma Alfred Worrell, and of Warren, alive.

In the Cemetery Road neighborhood, it was no secret that a cluster of nine or ten families had been squatting in the bush between the cemetery and the sprawling forest to the west. What young Madam Warren did not know was that back there in the forested squatters' community, on the bank of the ravine, was where Mister Harry had his . . . well, was where he stayed. Exactly where, nobody ever said.

Truth be told, Beatrice felt she was not really married. She and Mister Harry had never touched each other, and did not dwell together. She saw the man once a day, at dinnertime.

Now, more than ever, she looked forward to spending time at the cemetery, sitting on the nearby tree stump, talking with her husband and parents while her children ran and played on the open grounds.

She talked about the big mistake she had made in marrying the strange man who now had the *farseness* to demand that she stop visiting the cemetery. She felt no attraction to the man. And it was clear that he did not care in any way about her.

She was not even sure they were legally married. She and Warren had married in a church, but Pa Fred and Ma Mabel who were only trying to help, had to persuade a priest in a distant town to do a private ceremony at his house for her marriage to Mister Harry.

She had signed the papers. Mister Harry had left to get his birth certificate so he could sign the papers. She did not know if he had gone back to the priest.

BURDENSOME RULES

Shocked that the indifferent silent shopkeeper would even address them, customers in the shop couldn't believe the demand Ma Beatrice's new husband was barking at them.

"Stop calling my wife, Madam Warren! Call her Ma Beatrice!"

Completely out of place, the man then made a demand of Beatrice that was so ridiculous and absurd, the confused new bride deafened her ears to them. She had no concern about Mister Harry's absurd demand that she stop visiting the cemetery.

Because she did not assert her rights as shop owner, she did not know what to do about Mister Harry's third demand. Although the boys were young they enjoyed helping their Mama wait on customers in the shop. Mister Harry took over that responsibility and ruled that his new wife stay at home and away from the shop.

Protesting, Beatrice insisted that she had to get groceries from the shop to feed her sons.

Without even a glance at her, Mister Harry grumbled to no one in particular, that the village had enough food anybody could get for free; there was no need for her to be in the shop.

To feed her children, Ma Beatrice often reaped whatever she had in her backyard kitchen garden—green figs, pigeon peas, ochroes, ground provisions, bigan, sim, and sometimes tomatoes.

But she got her dried peas, dried beans, masala, flour, rice, and salt; her salt-fish, salt-beef, pig foot, pig tail, sugar, and milk; mayonnaise, her cooking oil, salt butter, and lard, her blue soap, brown soap, sweet soap, Vaseline, and blue; her cocoa, soft candle, matches, pitch-oil, cock set, thermogene, and tiger balm, from the shop.

It was hard for the mother to do without a regular supply of goods. And it was also hard for her to take care of her family without cash. She needed cash to pay for her ride to the market every Sunday morning. And she had to buy fish, or meat, for Sunday lunch. She also had to buy watercress, cabbage, beets, and carrots. No classy mother prepared Sunday lunch without fish or meat, a green salad, and diced beets and carrots mixed in mayonnaise.

But the man she had married couldn't care less about what she wanted, or how she felt. And he had no concern for her or her children's wellbeing. As long as she had a large meal for him at dinner time every day, he was satisfied.

Ma Beatrice was left to figure out for herself what this man she now called 'husband' wanted from her. It was clear that he didn't want her love, and he didn't want her house. It seemed that his only reason for agreeing to her proposal was to get her money, and to guarantee for himself daily, a large meal at evening time.

The backyard garden was small, so when one crop was harvested Ma Beatrice had to wait for another crop to grow. Throughout the village, however, and especially up there on the hill, neighbors shared whatever crop they had in abundance.

Several neighbors on Cyril Hill had breadfruit trees and coconut trees. Some of these trees bore throughout the year, so Ma Beatrice always had breadfruit and dry coconuts. With Mister Harry's new rules, she would be forced to make her own coconut oil, but never again could she prepare a tasty Sunday lunch for her family.

The new bride was so upset with herself for marrying the weird man, she sometimes hid from her sons and choked on her tears. Regardless of how he responded to her request for goods, the shopkeeper never honored the shopping list his wife placed on the shop counter.

Every evening after he had closed the shop doors at five-thirty sharp, Mister Harry went to the smaller room where he counted, and recorded, all the day's earnings. After locking away all cash in the metal safe, he exited through the narrow side door, and headed straight for the woman's dinner table.

DUTIFUL WIFE

Mister Harry had married a good woman, and she treated him as honorably as she had treated her beloved husband, Warren Bartelay.

At meal time she spread a smoothly ironed starched table cloth, on the table. She then set out a dish for each member of her family.

When she cooked soup, she set out a bowl for each of her sons, one for herself, and a larger one for Mister Harry, since he was the man of the house.

If she served solid food, like grains, ground provision, fruit vegetables—like breadfruit, plantain, or green figs, she set out a plate for each of her sons, one for herself, and always, a larger one for Mister Harry.

Ma Beatrice taught her sons to eat with a fork, except when they were having a liquid meal, like soup. They used a spoon to feed themselves any liquid meal. And they used a fork to feed themselves any meal served on a plate.

Mister Harry, however, ate all meals with a spoon—a large spoon. Ma Beatrice made sure to place that large spoon at her husband's place setting at dinnertime.

Every member of the family had their designated place at the table. Each boy sat on the same chair at every meal. Ma Beatrice sat at the end of the table, and Mister Harry sat at the head of the table.

When her beloved husband was alive, the young wife used her china wares only on special occasions. For everyday meals she used her lovely patterned enamel cups, plates, and bowls.

No more!

Now, as a matter of habit, she served dinner in her finest china ware—wedding gifts to herself and Warren.

Never could she sit at table with her family without recalling how tirelessly Warren had worked late into many nights, at his workbench at the back of the house, building that sturdy, long dining table. Calvin and Joshua also remembered.

At dinner time the devoted mother would place a large bowl of steamed provision at the center of the table. Most of the time it was breadfruit, or green fig, but sometimes she had ground provision—depending on what she had reaped from her garden or what a neighbor had shared with her.

In addition to the bowl of provision she would have another large bowl with a meat or vegetable stew. Sometimes it was callaloo or stewed peas. Even stewed green mangoes at times.

Of course, if a neighbor killed a goat, or a pig, Ma Beatrice was sure to get a piece of goat meat or a piece of pork, for her pot. Very rarely a farmer might kill a young heifer. Then she would get enough veal for a meal.

Also, when the hunters came back to the village with a deer, a porcupine, a couple manicou, iguana, or tattoo, they would cut up the meat and share a few pieces with Warren Bartelay's widow. Sometimes Robert or Pa Fred would drop off some warbines or cascadura from the ravine, in her kitchen.

There were some items Ma Beatrice had to get from the shop, however. Gathering her courage, she stopped asking Mister Harry for some salt, sugar, oil, flour, condensed milk, or kerosene, or matches.

Whatever response he grumbled, always meant 'no'; so, Ma Beatrice would boldly go to the shop and take what she needed. Ignoring his scowling averted eyes, she would take down from the shelves whatever she wanted.

Despite his indifference to the woman he had once referred to as 'his wife', the strange man was always sure that a plate would be laid out for him at the dinner table every evening. And there would be a large mug of juice on the table.

He could not care less where at the table he had to sit. That he sat at the head of the table was purely Beatrice's doing.

The village did not have electricity, so residents relied on the ice truck that drove through outlying areas at least twice a week.

Ma Beatrice always kept a thermos packed with shaved

ice. When the children arrived from school every day they had a cold drink, but at dinner-time drinks were served at room temperature.

LOUTISH DINNER GUEST

The upper and lower halves of the wide wooden door opened directly onto the yard on the western side of the house. When the family sat for dinner, all eyes would be tensely focused on that open doorway.

At exactly the same time every evening, the unshaven man, wearing a dinged merino, would tramp up the four wooden steps into the dining room. With eyes latched onto the serving dishes at the center of the table, he would drag out his chair, plunk himself down, and proceed to shovel whatever quantity of food he wanted, onto his plate.

"Grace before meals" would have been said before his arrival.

After gobbling down every morsel he had shoveled from his plate into his moustached covered mouth, Mister Harry would then noisily guzzle down the tall glass of juice placed there for him.

Fed to full, with a loud drawn-out burp, and without even a grunt of recognition to anyone, he would shuffle through the door and be gone till the next evening.

The man's behavior was not unlike a dog licking its bowl clean and then going about its business.

ENOUGH IS ENOUGH

Fed up with the man's ill-mannered and selfish behavior, the thoroughly disgusted mother, without notifying him, changed dinnertime from five-thirty to four-thirty.

Tramping through the open door, the next evening, the man dragged out the chair, and was actually reaching for the serving dish when he realized that no food was on the table, and that not one family member was present.

Since, by his own self-imposed rules, he never talked to the woman he had once referred to as his wife, nor to her children, he could not call out to them or ask why they weren't having dinner.

An open doorway separated the dining room from the kitchen, the mother silently rationalized; the man knew where the kitchen was. If he wanted he could check the pot for leftovers. She couldn't care less. She was finding it very difficult to continue doing kind things for this man who showed not one iota of concern for herself or for her sons.

Warren's widow wished she didn't have to be around the weird man she had married and prayed he would immediately get a bus ride out of Tapara and out of her life. If only, she thought, he would take a hint and stop appearing in her house!

Because she did not put two and two together, Ma Beatrice could not comprehend what happened once she stopped providing dinner for Mister Harry.

NIGHTLY KITCHEN RAIDS

Even before she had fled to her old home at the top of Cemetery Road she could not understand why she would lock up at nights before going to bed, yet get up in the morning to find a door or a window wide open.

And whatever food she would have left out the night before, would be gone.

There were no beggars in her village. And anyhow, beggars were mild-mannered, humble, older people. They never broke into homes.

Very slowly, they would hobble through the village, with their stick and grimy long sack, enter every yard to beg, and after a day or two be gone with bags heavier with pennies, cents, and maybe a stale rock cake or a stale hops bread.

The people of Tapara looked out for one another.

When neighbors on the slope became aware that

something strange was going on at Beatrice's house at nights, they started *throwing an eye* at the house before they locked up for the night.

To his wife, Mister Harry was an enigma. Nothing she said seemed to matter to him. She felt it was pointless to even mention anything about the break-ins to him.

Why he hung around her house and shop she did not understand.

LAGAHOO, YOU THINK?

Late one night, Pa Fred, whose house was two house lots down from Beatrice's home, on the eastern side of the slope, had seen a large dog ambling away from Ma Beatrice's kitchen, heading for the shop.

Every human resident on the hill could identify every dog that belonged up there. Pa Fred was sure this animal was a stray.

Word quickly spread that the nightly intruder in Ma Beatrice's house was a dog. Calvin vowed to look out for the nightly intruder.

One humid August night, early in the first quarter of the moon, Calvin had been tossing and turning so much, he got out of bed and threw open both halves of the wooden window. About four yards ahead, just beyond the open back porch in the poor visibility darkness, a low branching roucou tree shaded the southern wall of Pa Manny's two bedroom thatched-roof house.

The wire-netting fence enclosing Beatrice's yard, ran past the roucou tree down along the northern boundary to the gate which led onto the slope.

The preteen was standing in front the wide-opened window, gazing up at the north star, when he thought he heard a grunt. Squinting in the dark, the boy poked his head out the window but drew it back in fast.

Glancing at the clock as he rushed to rouse his brother, he noted that the time was eleven o'clock.

Everyone had been in bed since seven o'clock. Across the yard, by Mister Robert's house, everything was quiet. Not a sound, not even a snore.

"Joshua! Joshua!" Calvin called softly to his younger brother on the low full-size bed. "Get up! Get up! Come and see what is coming out of the kitchen!"

The younger boy rubbed his eyes as he bolted to the window. Squinting, he peered across the narrow open space to the open back porch that led to the kitchen door.

Overhead, bright stars twinkled in the blackness, and the first quarter moon shone just enough to allow him to see what had alarmed Calvin.

"Where that big pig come from?" The boy watched the animal curiously as it wobbled down the four treads on the back step, at the eastern end of the house, and turned to leave the way it must have entered, along the four-foot path between the fence and the kitchen.

By this time, nine-year-old Canaan was up.

Calvin quietly left the room and hastily returned, gripping

a broomstick. Joshua crept into his mother's room, quietly opened the hump-back trunk, and in no time, with his Papa's brown leather belt in hand, rejoined his brothers.

As soon as his older brothers had lowered themselves onto the ground outside, Canaan, as instructed, gently closed back both halves of the window.

The boys moved carefully towards the kitchen door. It was ajar. Who had unlatched it, they did not know. Quickly latching it back from inside, they hurried back to their room, and had just cracked the window open when they again heard a grunt.

Because this part of the house was L-shaped, the boys could see the hog as it wobbled back up the steps, apparently again heading for the kitchen, without it seeing them approaching from behind.

"Get out!" Calvin softly screamed in the dark, and he jabbed the broomstick against the side of the large pink creature. "Get out of my house! Out! Out! Out!"

Just in time he jumped back and away from the animal's vicious swing towards him. Grunting menacingly, the determined hog again swung its snout towards the older boy only to be momentarily tumbled as the belt in Joshua's upraised hand, in full force, connected with its head. Berserk with rage, the animal swiftly was back on its feet, lunging towards Joshua, but utterly confused by Calvin's stout and ready defense of his brother, the startled animal with the speed of a light weight creature, sprinted out of the house, out of the yard, down the slope, and up Cemetery Road, squealing all the way.

Early the very next morning, Pa Manny, his son, Robert, and Pa Fred, met the boys, barefooted, sitting on the floor of their back porch, listlessly swinging their legs over the well-swept yard, and looking lost and miserable.

"What is the matter, boys? What happened last night?" Robert asked.

"Something is wrong, Mister Robert", Calvin moaned. "We had to chase a big hog out of our kitchen."

"A hog?" Pa Fred looked puzzled. "It wasn't the dog?"

"No. It was a hog." While Pa Fred was dealing with his confusion over the identity of the creature, Calvin moaned, "That hog was not a hog, Pa Fred. Joshua and I feel we should not have hit it."

"Not a hog?" All three men blurted out.

"What do you mean, Calvin?" Pa Fred prodded Warren's first son for clarification.

"Pa Fred, the kitchen door was wide open. When we first spotted the animal, it was coming out of our kitchen. A hog can't open the kitchen door. We had latched it from inside. Still, I feel we should not have hit that creature."

"You feel you should have left it alone?" Robert tried to understand how the boy was feeling.

"I don't know, Mister Robert. I feel confused", Calvin griped.

"Pa Fred, I can understand how the boys feeling. What you

think going on here?"

"I am listening, Robert. Listening and thinking. What you think, Manny?"

"Like you, Fred, I'm listening and thinking. And wondering."

"I feel frightened, Pa Fred." Joshua's wide-opened eyes searched the older man's face for any assurance that he and his brother would be safe. "I tell you that hog was not a hog. It did not move like a hog. If you hit a hog it should run away. That animal was trying to hurt Calvin. I had to hit it hard. That was the only way to prevent it from hurting Calvin."

"You should see how it sprinted out of here. It was almost sailing through the air", Calvin's eyes opened wide as he maneuvered his hands to simulate how the hog sailed through the air as it sprinted downhill.

"H'mm", the adults muttered in chorus, gazing intently at the boy.

Walking away from the shop, the men lingered in front Pa Manny's house.

"LaGahoo, you think, Fred?" Pa Manny quizzically stared at the older man.

"It looks so, Manny." Pa Fred's expression was pensive.

"LaGahoo?" Robert laughed. "That is like saying the story about the frog turning into a Prince was true."

"Suppose it was true, Robert?" Pa Fred peered over his spectacles and gazed unblinkingly at the young man. "Suppose that story was true?"

BEATRICE FLEES

Early one fore-day morning Ma Beatrice stepped out of her bedroom, in the southwestern corner of the roomy house, walked diagonally across her rectangular living room, and was about to walk past the kitchen to check on her sons, when she heard an unusual sound.

Slowly opening the kitchen door, she felt cool night air sweeping into her kitchen. Alarmed, because she had latched that open window shut before going to bed, she looked around and saw the large dog Pa Fred had described, with its head in her soup pot.

Quietly grabbing her thermos bottle of ice cold water packed with shaved ice, she snuck up behind the canine intruder, and swiftly emptied the thermos onto its back. The squealing dog spun around, rammed its snout against her belly and bolted out the window, onto the slope.

Terrified by the shock attack, Beatrice nevertheless quickly hauled in her window and then limped back to her bed, holding her belly.

Later that morning Ma Cyril examined the suffering woman's belly. No bruise was visible, but the pain was unrelenting.

Not one night had passed since she had stopped feeding Mister Harry that the hog or the dog had not raided Ma Beatrice's kitchen. The young mother became afraid of the creature and with good reason, because whenever she tried to chase it away, it rammed its snout against her belly, hurting her all over again.

Although she could cite no basis for her conviction that Mister Harry had something to do with the dreadful animals harassing her home, Beatrice, nevertheless felt that he knew everything about what was happening to her. Pa Fred felt the same way.

They both thought it strange that the dog and the hog never appeared together. And neither animal was ever seen in the day. One or the other animal appeared only at nights. And it did not bother any other family. And from all accounts whether it was the hog or the dog, the animal, after speeding down Cyril Hill, and bolting up Cemetery Road, always disappeared back of the cemetery.

Before Beatrice had married Mister Harry, some villagers in the outskirts of the village used to complain about a hog raiding their kitchen at nights. Sometimes it was a dog.

Ma Rufina had told her son, Kenneth, that members of their church from different parts of the island used to talk about those kitchen raiding creatures. But it had been many years since she had heard anybody complain about them.

With Pa Fred's help, the young mother started putting two

and two together. Still, however, since she couldn't identify the real problem, she couldn't find a solution.

Beatrice felt she couldn't take the harassment anymore. The final straw for her was the scare she got early one morning.

Hearing an unusual noise in her kitchen, she had tiptoed across her living room, quietly opened the door to the kitchen, and from a safe distance, peeped into her kitchen. Sure enough, there was the creature leaping through the window, on its way out. Nervously, she had pulled in her window, and latched it. Then she collapsed on the kitchen floor in sobs.

She was fed up, tired of having to hide from the animal in her own house.

Pa Fred wondered where the creature had come from. He had his suspicions but held his tongue out of fear of terrifying Beatrice even more.

Daily, the young mother lived in dread that the creature might attack her sons. Ever since that first attack, she had been nursing a sore belly. Enough was enough. She was taking her children and getting out of that haunted house.

Before the breaking of day, she got her children out of bed and told them they were moving to the old family house. Together they packed boxes with only what the family absolutely needed.

With Pa Fred's help, she had located Natty, one of her former admirers who had to step aside when she accepted Warren's proposal. Natty came with his jitney and transported the mother and sons, and their many boxes, to her parents' old house at the top of Cemetery Road.

Mister Harry was at a loss, and so were most of the neighbors, when they realized that Beatrice had abandoned her house.

But Pa Fred quietly spread word that Beatrice was forced to abandon her home to escape the harassing creature that rammed its snout against the sore spot on her belly whenever it confronted her in her house.

COMMUNITY CARING

Neighbors were glad Beatrice had moved far away from the uncaring man. And though nobody understood the link between Mister Harry and the animal that was like a plague in Beatrice's household, neighbors felt that Mister Harry had something to do with the creature harassing Beatrice.

Mothers in the immediate neighborhood were very concerned about how the young mother was going to feed her family now that she had fled far away from her kitchen.

Pa Worrell's old house had a broken down detached kitchen on the eastern side; but it had nothing for his daughter to cook with, and nothing to cook.

Almost immediately five mothers from Lower Tapara came up with a plan to take turns supplying Beatrice with dinner every day till they could get her back into her house. They agreed to do this for Pa and Ma Alfred, and for their beloved Warren.

Each mother, when it was her turn, would have her son deliver dinner for the family.

On returning home from school, the boy would do his

chores, then set out, basket in hand, on the long walk to Upper Tapara.

Depending on how much work a boy had to complete after school, and the distance he had to walk, sometimes he got to Ma Beatrice long before the sun went down. At other times a boy got there just as it was getting dark.

To everyone's astonishment, and horror, within a week of Beatrice moving to her old family house, the dog was seen ambling towards her new location.

But because the animal appeared only at night, if the boy carrying dinner arrived long before dark, the family ate in comfort and the boy returned home unmolested.

Occasionally, if a boy was late, instead of walking along the road, he would do like village hunters—pass through the bush that extended back of the houses at the upper end of Cemetery Road; then he would approach Ma Beatrice's house from the back.

If a boy approached the house from the road, after the sun had gone down, the family was almost certain to go to bed hungry that night; unless, a boy was accompanied by his father, or by young Jonathan, the body builder.

For some strange reason, the animal never bothered Jonathan.

AVOIDING FOREST FIRE

So as not to be totally dependent on neighbors for food, Beatrice explored the forest behind the house for Lisbon yams. To her pleasant surprise, sure enough, plants from her childhood days had survived.

Almost daily, the family enjoyed roasting yams on a fire in a clearing near the little outside kitchen.

Knowing however, how easily a fire could spread in the forest, for extra precaution, the mother always made sure the fire was thoroughly put out.

Even when the last flame was doused, if Beatrice saw a little hot smoke rising out of some embers, she soaked the ashes with another *pitch-oil tin* of water.

DOG DEMANDING DINNER

Residents at the upper end of Cemetery Road were at a loss to comprehend why the strange dog, every evening, hung around Beatrice's home for dinner.

Tapara village-pots were savory. They smelt appetizing and they were *finger-lickin* tasty.

Mothers in the village, like most village mothers anywhere, had '*sweet hands*'. You could smell their pots from far off, and after you were through eating a plate of their food or a bowl of their soup, like the strange dog, you wanted to lick the plate or the bowl clean.

But even though steam from tasty pots blew about in the neighborhood, the strange dog seemed drawn only to Beatrice's yard.

Thirteen-year-old Kenneth raced with the setting sun but he delivered dinner sent by his mother, Ma Rufina, before the dog appeared.

Under the glow of a bottle flambeau inside, and with a new moon covering outside in darkness, the family was enjoying the spicy oil down when Ma Beatrice rigidly pushed her plate aside and stood upright. Her boys turned troubled eyes towards her.

Kenneth listened, and understood. A low growl was circling the old board house.

Concerned that the animal might try getting into the house through the front door, the boy asked Calvin to help him stack some boxes against the old wooden door with bottom and upper halves.

The growling intensified even as the boys pushed boxes of clothing and pots and dishes behind the door.

Kenneth was hearing his mother's voice as he urged Ma Beatrice to forget about the dog, and eat. Ma Rufina had said to him, "I did not prepare this breadfruit and salt beef oil-down for that nuisance of an animal to gobble down".

The food was still piping hot, so the aroma of tasty salt beef flavored with fresh green seasonings, lay heavily in the house and swirled out into the air outside, tantalizing the animal's taste buds.

The canine growled, and snarled, and furiously scratched at the door. The frightened children, with plates in their hands, huddled close to their mother who was too terrified to eat.

Determined to get her children out before the dog scratched its way in, the frightened mother, assisted by the older boys, grabbed her torchlight and quickly helped Canaan, and

Elijah, out the window.

Crouching in the bush, Warren's widow held his children close. She wished she could stop the flow of the little boys' tears, but she could not even stop the flow of her own.

Wrapped in the new moon darkness, the family endured the howling and snarling, and the sound of pushing and scratching till the old door gave way.

They all recognized the sound of cardboard boxes tumbling across the floor.

Angry and frustrated, Ma Beatrice listened till the chomping ceased and the large canine, grunting almost like a hog, ambled out along the track to Cemetery Road.

The mother ached for relief.

A SON ATTACKED

It was Ma Mabel's turn to prepare a meal for Ma Beatrice and her boys. Although at five feet four inches, Telbut's mother weighed just about one hundred and ten pounds, the villagers knew she was no light weight.

A widow, she had to be tough to be able to fend for herself and her son.

A rumor was sweeping through the village. People were saying that Ma Mabel had a plan for the ole dog. But nobody knew what that plan was.

None of the boys in on the plan told Kenneth because his mother, Ma Rufina, might not have agreed to it.

Ma Rufina was a godly woman who believed in being kind, even to animals. But as Ma Mabel told the boys, sometimes you have to fight fire with fire.

Early one morning, Ma Mabel sent Telbut to the shop for six cents worth of black pepper. In those days that was plenty black pepper. Groceries were cheap.

Leaving his *washykongs* home, barefooted, the young teenager ran out his yard, turned south on the narrow asphalt road, and swung around the bend. Because the pitch was hot, he played hopscotch between the pitch road and the grassy roadside as he raced around the big bend on Cemetery Road, and dashed across the road.

In the shop at the top of Cyril Hill, Mister Harry wrapped the black pepper corns in a piece of brown grocery paper, then curiously glanced at Telbut, and probed, “Ma Mabel buying plenty black pepper?”

“She’s going to make a special recipe for the greedy ole dog”, Telbut grinned.

Mister Harry watched the wiry energetic boy hard on the sly.

That evening Telbut, having walked more than two miles to deliver the dinner his mother had prepared for the family, went past the nuisance canine just after the sun had gone down.

The creature growled and snarled in the waxing gibbous moonlight, but Telbut stared it in the eyes and walked on.

Strange enough, the animal did not jump the boy, but when Telbut reached Ma Beatrice’s house, down at the end of the grassy track, the dog was right behind him.

Ma Beatrice and her hungry children watched the dog on

their steps and the bag still in Telbut's hand, and they froze; but the unflappable boy stood calmly in the doorway.

Keeping his back to the canine, Telbut took a large bowl out of the bag and handed it to Ma Beatrice.

Fearfully, the mother placed the bowl of delicious smelling food on the table next to the window.

Ignoring a warning growl behind him, the boy again reached into his bag. This time he took out a smaller bowl, turned around, and placed it on the floor in front the animal.

Snarling, the dog jumped the boy. Bowl and boy were sent tumbling.

Desperate to snatch the family's dinner from the chomping mouth, Telbut scrambled to his feet, dashed out into the early night, and was soon aiming a stick at the canine's back.

Fearfully, Beatrice and her children retreated to a far corner.

Before the stick could make contact with its target, the canine intruder again swung around and charged into the fourteen years-old.

Small-boned and wiry, Telbut was sent sprawling, for the second time that evening. This time however, he stumbled backward through the open doorway onto the shaky wooden landing.

When minutes later, Ma Beatrice carried the flambeau close to the boy to find out why his back was burning so much, she saw a long, deep scratch.

Honoring the brave boy's request, the stressed-out young mother packed salt in the wound.

Ma Mabel trembled with rage when she heard how the creature had attacked her son. She vowed to get that animal.

FRIGHTENING DOG!

Villagers kept themselves informed about Ma Beatrice's family. As was their custom, they gathered in the big yard in front Mister Harry's shop to talk. And they talked mostly about Ma Beatrice's hard life with her cruel husband.

Although they were disgusted with Mister Harry the people dared not talk too loudly because they didn't want the hard-hearted shopkeeper to hear them.

Not that they were afraid of him, but they felt he hated Ma Beatrice so much he might claim he didn't have whatever items they needed from his shop, if he thought they were sympathetic to his wife.

Playing it safe, the neighbors gathered outside the shop and whispered. And while they whispered, the shopkeeper *strained his ears* to hear what they were saying.

Once he heard one of the mothers saying to another, "***A 'A,*** Madam McLeod, but *dat's de* strangest *ting ah ever see*—like *de man* put obeah on Warren's family!"

Another time he heard, "But *allyuh ent* notice something

about *dat* dog? It is always raiding only Ma Beatrice's kitchen, just like *de* hog."

"Dog?" Pa Fred had just stepped away from his house and was about to walk down the slope when he heard the ladies talking about the creature.

He adjusted the battered old felt hat on his head, then turned and faced the ladies. "Dog, *allyuh* say? Hah, hah. *Dat ent* no dog. *Dat is* a dawg!

"Why *dat* creature *doh* try raiding my kitchen at nights? Eh? Hah! *Monkey know which tree to climb, oui!"*

And sixty-five-year-old Pa Cyril Fred, frustrated because so far all his attempts to protect Alfred Worrell's daughter and grandsons, had been failing, sauntered down the hill, every step weighted with concern for Beatrice and her boys.

From up there in his shop, Mister Harry heard Pa Fred loud and clear.

NEIGHBORHOOD WOES

Several boys, their well-oiled feet protected either in sapats or alpagatas, were standing on the cool pitch road in front Kenneth's yard. They were talking about Calvin's family.

"You going early this evening, Kenneth?" fourteen-year-old Stefan asked.

Villagers could make out Stefan from a distance because of how he stood with his shoulders back and his head held high. Like most of the boys in the village, he also had been attacked by that dog. Sometimes he had outsmarted it, and one time it had knocked him down and gulped down the food he had walked one and a half miles to deliver.

After hearing what Pa Fred had said about the animal, the boys stopped talking about the 'dog'. They changed the pronunciation from dog to 'DAWG'!

Kenneth had swept his front yard while his friends chatted in front his house on the quiet deserted road that branched off Cemetery Road. Still holding the *cocoyea broom*, he declared, "This is one evening that dawg would have to go hungry. You should see how Calvin's family *freeze up* when they hear that animal outside."

"My mother says the dawg thinks like a man", Errol quipped. "Aye Kenneth, Ma Rufina must be get vexed when she heard you had to run and leave that food, eh? Why you don't wait for your father to walk with you to Ma Beatrice?"

"Pa comes home late. I can't keep Calvin and his family waiting so long. Anyhow, I am leaving early today."

"My father can't walk since he fell from that ladder." Winston sounded sad. "But I get home early enough from Commercial lessons to leave long before the dawg comes out.

"On my days, Calvin and them don't have to rush to eat. And Ma Beatrice, Calvin, Joshua, Canaan, and Elijah walk back with me half of the way sometimes.

"You know how excited Nazir gets when he sees any of us! Sometimes we have to stop and play with him a little bit when we passing his house."

"Aye, Winston", Errol chuckled, "that little boy likes to play 'Catch', *eh?* And he can run so fast with that little short leg!"

"Whenever I walk past Ma Raheeman's yard", Telbut smiled, "Nazir runs out to talk with me. I feel sorry when I see him hopping about with that little crooked leg. Ma says he had polio".

"Aye, Winston, when your father fell off that ladder that had to be pain *fuh so, eh*?" Errol looked sympathetically at Winston. "What part of his body got hurt?"

"Nerves in his spine," Winston sighed. "He is always begging God to let him walk again. Pa always repeating prayers for healing—morning, noon, and night. And in between. He is always mumbling some prayer."

"Ma says God answers prayers", Kenneth reflected.

"Maybe. But it is almost six years Pa praying for healing."

"Winston", Jonathan, the fourteen-year-old body builder turned to the almost sixteen-year-old, "I think it is better to pray than not to pray. Either God answers prayers or God doesn't answer prayers. If God does answer prayers, who's to say that God wasn't about to answer your father's prayers just when you were thinking he had been praying too long?"

Winston listened to his fourteen-year-old friend. "I suppose you have a point there, Jonathan", he conceded.

"I think it would be unfair though", Jonathan mused, "for Pa Ali to have to live the rest of his life like a cripple because of one small accident. How old is your father, Winston?"

"Only forty", the boy replied.

"My mother prays out loud sometimes", Telbut interjected. "At any time she would suddenly bawl out, 'Lord, stop that creature from harassing Beatrice and her sons!'."

"Winston", Kenneth felt he had to tell Winston what he had learned about being patient with God, "You said Pa Ali has been praying for healing about six years now? Well, my mother belongs to a prayer group that has been praying for a man who disappeared before all of us born."

"What you mean, 'disappeared'? Jonathan asked.

"Ma said, one day the boy—he was just twenty-two years old--was in his house and the next day he wasn't there."

"*Jus so*?" fourteen-year-old Stefan blurted out.

"*Just so*", Kenneth replied. "It is more than twenty years since this man missing. Ma says if you meet the lady they say he wanted to marry, you would swear that this man is still alive somewhere. People in the prayer groups really believe God will answer their prayers. Ma said the lady knows that God will bring this man back to her."

"After all this time? If he comes back to her he would be an old man. She must really love the man", Jonathan mused. "You know the man's name?"

"Abe Chavier", Kenneth replied.

THE BOYS' PLAN

Errol looked at the zippered lunch bag Jonathan was carrying. "What you have in that bag, Jonathan?" Errol asked curiously. “You carrying that for Ma Raheeman?”

“My mother is sending bush medicine for catarrh for Pa Raheeman”, Jonathan replied. “I am glad all of you are coming with me.”

“Catarrh?” Telbut looked surprised. “Sometimes I really hear Pa Raheeman hawking and coughing when I pass their house.”

“How is that bad scratch you got on your back, Telbut?” Winston asked. “We could see it? Aye, that is a long scar. It still hurts?”

“Sometimes it swells up. The doctor said some splinters dug into my flesh when my back hit the landing that night. Sometimes it bothers me and sometimes I don’t remember it. But I don’t like knowing I’m walking around with wood splinters in my back.” Telbut looked pensive.

“I wonder what that dawg has against Ma Beatrice”,

Jonathan muttered thoughtfully. "And when would the harassment stop?"

"The shameful thing is that even though Mister Harry owns a shop, his family is hungry most of the time. I feel that man is not normal. Something must be wrong with him", Winston opined.

"Aye, when children have problems look how it affects them in school", Jonathan quipped. "Calvin's teacher complained that Calvin fidgets in class. The boy failed fifth standard when everybody else went up to a higher class".

"If I had to live like Calvin, they might have kept me down in school also", Winston noted. "The whole family is *under too much pressure*. Aye, it's hard for anybody to concentrate on school books when they under so much pressure".

The boys delivered the bag to Ma Raheeman and were heading back home.

"So what we going to do, *fellahs*?" Errol voiced eveyone's common concern. "Nothing will change unless we do something different. The problem with that animal is that it is fixated on getting dinner from Ma Beatrice. We have to find a way to shift its focus away from Ma Beatrice and her children."

"So", said Jonathan, "we have to come up with a plan that involves dinner. And it must be a knock-out plan. But we can't do it by ourselves."

"What about talking it over with Ma Mabel?" asked Winston. "Your mother is the one person I feel sure could help us stop that creature, Telbut."

The boys decided to pool their ideas. When they were satisfied that they had come up with a great strategy they would go to Ma Mabel.

That was their plan.

TO STOP THE CANINE

Several months had passed since the animal's attack on Telbut. This Friday morning, Ma Mabel was out of bed earlier than usual. Her mind was heavy. This was the day to execute the boys' plan.

Telbut and his friends had come to her with a plan. They were adamant that they had to make this plan work. There could be no room for failure. And it had to be implemented while the moon was in the waxing gibbous or full moon phase.

On most afternoons the boy assigned to deliver meals to Ma Beatrice's family hurried home from school so he could get to Ma Beatrice before the animal appeared. Sometimes, however, a boy had so many chores to complete that by the time he reached the entrance to the track, the fearsome creature was already there.

Sitting on a low small stool, in her detached tapia-walled kitchen, Ma Mabel dragged out the *Sill*, a large flat stone, and the *lorha*—a smaller, cylindrical stone used as a rolling pin; then she tied a thick linen scarf around her face to cover her nose.

After knotting the scarf securely behind her head, she took out a cup of black pepper corns from a can on the kitchen counter, and with the lorha, ground all the black pepper corns on the Sill. She ground all of it to a fine powder.

The healthy, slender lady then stretched her firm arm across the tapia counter-top and pulled a large jar of salt towards her.

Diligently, her son, Telbut, had gone about his chores that morning. With the rising of the sun, he had been toting buckets of water from the standpipe out on the road, to fill the three barrels at the side of the house.

He had swept the yard, and had gathered all the trash and hauled it off to the spot in the backyard to be burned. And he had dumped the week's collection of empty bottles, empty condensed milk cans, empty Vienna sausage cans and sardine cans in the dump heap in the bush at the back.

The boy had been urging his mother to execute his friends' plan. It was a tight plan. No loop holes. And he insisted that it be executed while the moon was waxing brighter at night.

Friday was the last school-day of the week. The neighborhood was fed up with the boldness of that dog.

Up there in his shop, the tallish unkempt unshaven shopkeeper, with muscular arms hanging from the sides of his dinged merino, *strained his ears* to hear what his customers were whispering out in the yard.

Because Warren Bartelay had built the shop at the top of a rocky incline, standing in the shop, surly Mister Harry had a clear view of the slope as it reached down to the road.

Luckily for him, the houses on the eastern side of the hill blocked his view of Cemetery Road as it extended around the foot of the massive hill. He might have been worried had he seen the clusters of neighbors chatting here and there on the road this morning.

On the hill, a few neighbors stepped away from their front yard to huddle and share the latest news.

The curious shopkeeper wondered what was happening. Nobody shared information with him so he was left to just wonder. He even tried *to pick some customers' mouths,* but the unfriendly man was *left in the dark.*

TEENS ON A MISSION

It was Telbut's turn again to deliver food to the distressed mother and her young sons. Pa Fred, who had been filling the void left by the death of Alfred Worrell, as a father figure in Tapara, felt more responsible than many for taking care of Beatrice and her children.

Like all villagers who remembered Pa and Ma Worrell and the beloved Warren Bartelay, he wanted Warren's family safely back in the house Warren had left them. So, as one of the seniors in on the plan, he had visited with Telbut and his mother and had suggested that Telbut get up early that Friday morning and do his chores.

The boy could then start out for Ma Beatrice's home as soon as he returned from school.

Winston had suggested to the other boys that all of them should be close to Ma Beatrice's house not only before the animal appeared, but even before Telbut arrived.

Telbut would not be left alone to carry out the group's plan. Besides, Telbut could not tote everything they would need at the house.

Ma McLeod was responsible for preparing dinner for the family this evening. She would send the food by her son, Stefan.

Staying with their plan, before they reached the houses at the upper end of Cemetery Road, the boys turned west, off the road, across a 'bandon; then they walked south, along the track that passed back of the high bush bordering the road. This track ran roughly parallel to Cemetery Road.

Ever since the young mother had moved to her old home, Natty had been picking up her boys on mornings, along with other school children nearby, to transport them to their school about three miles away.

After school, she walked down about a half mile to collect her boys.

This evening, the teens on a rescue mission deposited their load in her kitchen before she returned home with her sons. Jonathan also filled the two pitch-oil tins with water from the standpipe on the road.

At four thirty sharp, Telbut had exited his yard and started on his walk south, up Cemetery Road. His house was farther away from Ma Beatrice's house than was Mister Harry's shop. Undetected by the shopkeeper, however, he walked past Cyril Hill, and then past the graveyard on his right.

Some of the younger children were terrified to walk alone, past the graves. Some would never point at anything in the graveyard because they believed that if they did, the finger they pointed with would rot and fall off.

Telbut had no such fears. With a zippered lunch bag in each hand, and a blazing sun overhead, the young teen strolled past the cemetery. And he strolled past the turn-off on the east, leading to Kenneth's home. Kenneth was not in on this evening's plan.

Chirps, whistles, and tweets, streamed from far and near, on both sides of the road. Anxiously, the boy plodded on. So much depended on him this evening.

Yellow tail black birds, small ground feeding brown birds, shimmering green humming birds, doves, chickeechongs, corbeaux, and keskidees, sailed, hovered, dove, all doing their customary thing, as though indifferent to the boy tirelessly plodding along, carrying a zippered bag in each hand.

Through this Edenic land the young boy strolled, mentally identifying the sounds and whistles that amplified with his focus during that long walk.

Observing the silent display of colorful butterflies sailing from wildflower to wildflower, and occasional batey mamselles, like helicopters, hovering, taking off, and landing, Telbut smiled. Nature never stopped revealing its wonders, even if it was just the cacophonous sounds of the forest as every stride moved him closer to his friends, and to the execution of their plan.

Never pausing to rest, but maintaining the rhythm of legs moving in harmony with his weighted arms, he passed flowering mango trees edging the roadside, and sniffed the scent of ambarella (hog plums), and tonka beans floating out from deep in the bush. All this as mentally he rehearsed the instructions his mother had given him.

Finally, houses and yards, and people, were before him. Destination was near. He had reached upper Tapara Village.

Up here among the few neighbors, expectation was running high. People were walking about in their yards and on the road. Now and then a neighbor called out to the boy with a bag in each hand.

Villagers watched, from the shade of fruit trees in their yard, and one or two from their front gallery, as Telbut passed by.

The people had heard of the dog's attack on the boy months earlier. Knowing Telbut's mother, the neighborhood expected that Ma Mabel would find a way to get even with that dog. She wasn't taking that attack on her son, so!

Word had spread that this day was again Telbut's turn to carry dinner for the family.

Now and then, as Telbut walked past, he heard some persons quietly call out, "Aye, Telbut". For the most part, however, the people just stood quietly in their yard, or sat quietly in their gallery, and watched the almost-fourteen-year-old approvingly.

Children who were running about the yards, playing their games, stopped and gazed as the boy passed by.

Silently affirming that this day would be the last that the creature would attempt to harass Ma Beatrice, the boy was walking past Ma Raheeman's house when her grandson, Nazir, a favorite in the community, limped up to the teen and whispered, "Telbut, I wish the dog would stop bothering Elijah's family".

"Me too", Telbut replied.

With the friendly neighbors behind him, the young friend of Ma Beatrice's family pushed on for the next half mile before he was in sight of the little two-bedroom house just off the road to the west.

As soon as Stefan saw Telbut approaching the house, as was planned, he left his friends on the track at the back of the houses and exchanged the basket his mother had sent for the family for the bag Ma Mabel had prepared for 'the boys'.

The evening sun was still high up in the sky as Ma Beatrice opened her door and welcomed the brave boy. After carefully placing the bags on the table, she gave the boy a wet cloth to wipe his face, and suggested that he take some time to catch his breath.

But Telbut left the family alone to enjoy the dinner Ma McCleod had prepared for them, and he went off, as pre-arranged, to join his friends and rehearse their plan for the evening.

Sitting in the bush back of the house, each boy remembered again why he felt so endeared to Ma Mabel. She had packed enough coconut bake and bigan choka so each of them could have their fill. And she had sent them the thermos of frozen lime squash concentrate they had been expecting.

Unknown to Ma Beatrice, while she and her family enjoyed

their early dinner, Telbut and his friends were in the back also enjoying their dinner.

All the boys, even Winston and Jonathan, who had to walk more than two miles to get home, would stay around till the plan was executed.

APPREHENSIVELY HOPEFUL

Everybody ate to their satisfaction. Calvin, twelve-year-old Joshua, eleven-year-old Canaan, and nine-year-old Elijah, were all tense, but at least this was one evening nothing was going to prevent them from enjoying the food a village mother had lovingly prepared for them.

Time was on their side, although this little family did not know how not to eat quickly.

All the mothers who took turns sending dinner for Ma Beatrice and her children were in their own way expressing loving support for the daughter and grandsons of Pa Alfred Worrell, and his devoted wife, Ma Elmina Worrell. And they were definitely standing up for their beloved Warren Bartelay as they tried their best to take care of his family!

After dinner, the family did as Telbut directed.

Ma Beatrice and Calvin went to the kitchen just outside the house. After lighting the coals they had heaped into the coal pot, they placed the large covered aluminum pot, filled with water, on the red hot coals.

Grabbing a piece of cardboard, Calvin fanned the coals into a glowing flame, and continued fanning till he could hear the water rumbling in a vigorous boil.

Ma Beatrice then emptied the quart can of soup concentrate Ma Mabel had sent her, into the boiling water. Her taste buds tingled as she sniffed the delicious aroma of hot split peas soup swirling in the air.

This pot of steaming hot soup would go in a corner away from the edge of the table so the steam could ooze through the crevices of the old house and land on the bony shelves of the creature's nasal cavities.

The creature would smell the pot and drooling, would be drawn into the house and to the food on the table.

That was the plan.

Meanwhile, inside, Telbut and Joshua had shut and latched the upper and lower halves of the wooden back door. They had also latched the window on the eastern side of the house—the side facing the road.

The hole for this window latch was shallow. With enough pawing and biting, the dog could spring open that window.

But Telbut was not worried about that happening.

The table was near this window. The pot of soup was under the edge of the table down from the window.

Telbut had walked with hammer and nails, and had properly secured the door the dog had damaged months before. Also, he had discovered two rusty latches on the upper edge of the upper door--one near the hinge, and the other on the far side of the door.

With swift movements the boys cleaned out the dusty holes in the upper frame, pushed in the door, and then tested it till they were sure it was secure. They then ran out to the detached kitchen to help Ma Beatrice fan the coal pot fire.

“That’s a loud bullfrog”, Ma Beatrice exclaimed as the bellow floated in on a rustling breeze.

Telbut smiled. He recognized Errol’s poor imitation of a bullfrog’s bellow. His friends were letting him know that they were observing from a distance.

They had faithfully delivered the coal-pot, coals, and soup pot, pot spoons, kitchen towels, and pot cloths, and thanks to body builder, Jonathan, Ma Beatrice had two pitch oil tins of water in her kitchen. And they had another pitch oil tin of water back there in the bush, for their lime squash.

Each boy had walked with his own cup made from empty condensed milk cans.

By ten minutes to six, Ma Beatrice, her sons, and Ma Mabel’s son, were inside the house, waiting.

Doors and windows were securely latched.

Mother and sons had been excitedly following Telbut's directions. Hope for an end to the animal's harassment was running high.

Everyone was feeling anxious, very anxious, and hopeful, very hopeful.

Ma Beatrice could not afford to stop and reason through how their elaborate preparations could end the harassment once and for all.

She just had to make herself believe that this night had to mark the end of this creature's harassment of her family.

Whatever Mister Harry had put this animal up to had to stop.

LURING THE CREATURE

Two young boys squeezed up next to each other, listening, as the hands of the clock on the table moved to six-thirty-five. And although a pale translucent darkness was settling outside as the sun withdrew its rays, already moon-glow was brightening up the night sky on this full moon night.

Ma Beatrice lit the flambeau and placed it on the table, against the wall; then she carefully lifted the large covered pot of soup and placed it on the floor in the corner away from the window.

She had to make sure that no quirkish accident could put her children at risk, so the pot was almost under the back of the table, near the wall.

Telbut reached into the one bag he had not yet unzipped. He took out a wide mouth thermos and placed it on the table next to the window; then he twisted the cover loose.

"Uhm, yum", Joshua licked his lips.

The aroma of crab and callaloo, and chicken stew, diffused throughout the room, and pulled on everybody's saliva.

More eyes than usual watched the large dog trot up the forested upper end of Cemetery Road at the usual time. Strolling villagers, seemingly taking a casual walk under the soft glow of a rising moon, cautiously crept closer towards the top of Cemetery Road where soft breezes rustled through heavy foliage on that very breezy evening.

Flavors of chicken stew, and crab and callaloo mixed with the strong aroma of split peas soup fanned briskly through the night air, skimming over bush and trees and soaring out to where the squatting creature waited.

Sniffing the air, the canine Mister Harry somehow seemed to be connected to, shifted to all fours, and vigorously shook itself.

After sniffing the air once more, the dog swung around and raced off towards the house, drooling all the way.

From the bush across from the window facing the road, illumined by the soft glow of moonlight, several shadowy figures watched. In the bright moonlight, one figure stood erect with shoulders firmly back, and head held high. Telbut's friends were staying close.

As the growls rumbled outside, Ma Beatrice stooped distressingly. Canaan and Elijah were already stooping anxiously behind stacks of boxes in the corner straight down and away from, the window.

Calvin wasn't about to let Telbut down. If Telbut could stand strong for his family, he would also stand strong.

Joshua hovered between standing with the two older boys and joining his younger brothers where they had already taken cover.

The animal was right there, right outside the house. Drawn by the tantalizing flavors still hanging heavy in the kitchen, it nosed around in desperate search of the food.

Finding no food, the snarling creature, berserk with desire, raced around the house, pausing only to growl at the front door and frantically paw at the window.

Telbut and Calvin stepped over to the table even as the barking and snarling bounced off the window. Ma Beatrice softly begged them to move away from the window and get out of sight.

Tantalized by flavor soaked vapors and steam seeping through cracks around the window, the animal wildly scratched and bit at the low window.

Telbut picked up the kitchen cloths and stooping under the table, carefully lifted the cover off the pot. He stuck a finger into the split pea soup but pulled it out fast as waves of steam billowed in the room and rushed through every crack and crevice in the walls.

He would endure the pain from his burned finger. Nothing he could do about that now.

Swiftly lifting the cover off the wide-mouth thermos, he felt his salivary glands watering as steam from the thermos rose to blend with the flavor of split peas soup swirling through the house.

Outside the window the canine lapped wildly at the air, and in no time, was on its hind legs, stretching to its full length while vigorously scratching at the window.

Shielded by stacks of boxes, Ma Beatrice pressed her elbows and knees onto the floor. Between her somewhat extended body and the wall, her young sons crouched.

Crouching exacerbated the pain at that sore part of her belly, but she had to live with that discomfort.

For a quick second the anxious mother glanced at the contents of the thermos. What she glimpsed was mouth-watering callaloo draped over yellow tom *tom balls*; and thick brown gravy covering grainy white rice.

The growling was right there, right outside the old wooden window awash with condensing vapors of the most delicious food. That was the window with a defective latch.

In her anxiety for the safety of her family, the distressed mother, now anxious about having that creature in the same room with her children, paid no more mind to the contents of the thermos; so she did not notice the two large golden-brown fish pies next to the tom tom balls.

Just how this food was supposed to free her family from being terrorized by the animal, she did not know.

Earlier, when she had poured the concentrate into the boiling water she did suspect that it was loaded with black pepper, but she would have never guessed what deterring ingredients Ma Mabel had carefully stuffed into each fish pie.

Although Beatrice did not know what plans Ma Mabel had put in place for this strange creature fixated on her family, with all the yearning she could muster, she prayed to be spared another encounter with the animal.

Her belly was still tender from the times the canine had deliberately rammed its snout into her. It was only God's mercies that she or her children had never been grabbed by the pointy teeth of that menacing creature.

Though terrified to have her family in the same room with the animal, she was doing all she could to cooperate with Telbut. She had warned her children that they had to be *as quiet as a mouse*.

Regardless of what happened, they could not alert the animal to their presence.

BOLD-FACED DOG

The drooling canine snarled and growled, and pawed and bit, as it struggled to pry the window open.With human-like grit, it tenaciously bit and pawed at the level of the yielding latch.

When it seemed that the window was about to be sprung open, Telbut, on Calvin's heels, softly dashed for cover.

Large pointed teeth, bathed in drool, rose above the grey old window sill as the growling head laboriously eased into the aroma soaked room.

At the sound of the deep-throated growl just a few feet away, a mother's hands muffled the screams of two young boys even as she stifled her own.

Jumping onto a sturdy little bench, the heavy creature swiftly planted its front paws on the sturdy old table. Without missing a beat, the large mouth was ravenously devouring every morsel in the thermos, lapping up the callaloo--even as the tom tom balls slid down its throat—and snatching the crispy fish pies.

In lightening succession, its powerful jaws chomped down,

first on one fish pie, then on the other.

Each stuffed with a delicate blend of one tablespoon of finely ground black pepper and one tablespoon of fine salt, the exploding fish pies tumbled the creature onto the floor, in a frenzied, gagging spin.

Wild with distress, the retching canine broke out of the frenzied spin, desperately swinging its large head from side to side, its bulging eyes frantically sweeping under the table.

In the glow of the flambeau, it spotted the pot of liquid, hidden away under the table. Gagging and tumbling, the quadruped plunged its large head into the pot of soup. Scorched, it pulled back hard, bathing its body in the blisteringly hot liquid.

From the bushes outside, several young figures stealthily stepped into the clearing and cautiously stared in the direction of the retching animal.

Out on Cemetery Road listening villagers heard the yowling and the howling, the retching and the yelping, and they itched to find out what was happening.

In a wink, Ma Beatrice lost her fright. The boys emerged from hiding and gazed in disbelief. Dumbfounded, Telbut just stared.

The creature had gotten more than any of them had bargained for. It all had happened so fast.

At one moment the canine was spinning around on the floor, yelping, sneezing, tumbling, retching and whining. The next moment it had leapt through the window, retching, and squealing as it tumbled along the moonlit track out to Cemetery Road.

Nearer to the village, men scampered to the side of the road. Women's gazes trailed off in amazement. Children ran to the front of their yards and just stared under the bright moon, at the retching, tumbling, gagging, rolling, squealing canine, slowly disappearing in the distance.

Everybody along that end of Cemetery Road saw the soaked, distressed quadruped lamely bolting, rolling, tumbling, down the road under the brilliant glow of a full moon.

And farther down in the village, Pa Fred and his wife, waited, as did Ma Mabel, to find out if their well-coordinated plan had worked after all.

Together, the boys tidied Ma Beatrice's house, and with their eyes on the path, they carefully picked their way through the bush as they headed home. Each hoped he had seen the last of the creature.

Some reported that the animal disappeared in the cemetery.

Next morning Mister Harry's shop was closed, and it stayed closed all day.

BLISTERED AND BANDAGED

It was again Telbut's turn to carry food for the family. The other boys walked with him. Every one of them carried a big stick, just in case the persistent intruder was again waiting for them. But nobody saw the creature that evening.

Talk in the village was about Telbut and how he had *fixed* the dawg. But Ma Mabel spread word that the plan had been *cooked up* by Winston and the other boys—well, all the boys except Kenneth, whose mother, Ma Rufina Millster, would not have agreed to cause distress to the animal in any way.

One week after the incident the shop opened; but Mister Harry wore dark shades and his face was wrapped from the crown of his head to his chin. On his nose, and around his mouth, people could see white ointment. And he wore a buttoned-up long-sleeved shirt.

Villagers could not understand what was happening. They were accustomed seeing Mister Harry in a sleeveless vest whenever he was in his shop. Now that his head was wrapped he looked very funny.

Mister Harry, himself, was at a loss to know what had

happened to his body. It had all been so sudden. The blisters and the pain. The doctor had asked how he got burned. He hadn't been burned. He and his doctor were both equally flummoxed.

If only he could recall how he spent his nights . . . if only.

He had a deep suspicion that some of the villagers had answers to his questions. but nobody talked to him about anything that was not on their grocery list.

Word reached Ma Beatrice about Mister Harry. She said she hoped that whatever was wrong with the man she had unfortunately married, would get him out of her life forever.

That spot on her belly--where the creature several times rammed its snout against her, was constantly sore. That was a pain she had to live with.

The neighbors felt that something inside her was damaged because of the tenderness she felt in that area of her belly.

"Mister Harry!" an alarmed Ma Rufina, who had gone to the shop with her son, Kenneth, stared in disbelief at the bandaged shopkeeper, "What happen to your face? And what happen to your eyes? Why you're covered up from head to toe!"

"Ma Rufina", the suffering man mumbled, "I came down—Achoo!" The man pulled out a small towel from his back pocket, and covered his mouth, "with this strange disease that have my whole body breaking out—Achoo! Achoo!—in blisters. Achoo! That was why I closed the shop."

"But Mister Harry", Kenneth, curious about Mister Harry's appearance and his sneezing, asked, "what happen? How come you sneezing so much?"

Mister Harry reluctantly answered the boy, "I walked around too exposed and catch the Achoo! And catch the cold."

Ma Ali, Winston's mother, was in shock when she saw Mister Harry's face. Placing the open palm of her right hand across her mouth, she stared in amazement at the shopkeeper before exclaiming, "But Mister Harry, what happen to your face?"

"Ma Ali", Mister Harry mumbled, "this strange disease I caught have my face breaking out in blisters."

Nobody felt sorry for Mister Harry because he had been so cruel to Ma Beatrice and her children. Besides, who had time to talk about the mean, hardhearted shopkeeper when there was more exciting news to talk about?

How Telbut took care of the dawg—that was the news!

The people were so relieved that Telbut had taken care of that nuisance of a creature they didn't seem to care whether or not Mister Harry overheard their conversations.

A couple weeks after the creature had stopped harassing the family, villagers were saying openly that Ma Beatrice and her children were starting to look so good since Telbut had gotten rid of that terror of an animal. It did not matter how many times they heard that a group of boys had come up with the plan that finally stopped the harassment.

As far as the people were concerned it was under Telbut's watch that the creature was stopped; so they persisted in saying that Telbut had stopped the harassment of Ma Beatrice and her sons.

Talk was that since Telbut had broken the jinx on the family nobody had seen the large dog or the large hog.

Mister Harry was right there behind his counter when just outside his door, the voice of an older man rang out, in a chuckle, as he addressed villagers standing around. "Aye, *allyuh*, this thing really strange, *yuh know*—that hog that sometimes showed up at nights, like it disappeared *jus so*! *Jus so*, boy.

"And the dog—aye, it is almost two months since Telbut fixed that animal. And like that disappear too. '*Jus so* those two animals just disappear, boy! *Jus so*! *Jus so*!"

And Mister Kaiser, the village building contractor, chuckled again as he entered the shop with his basket, and placed his list on the counter.

Villagers had stopped whispering around Mister Harry.

The distressed shopkeeper listened quietly as though he had no idea what the people were talking about.

And indeed, he had no idea.

A FRIGHTENED MAN

Ma Mabel, with slow determined steps, mounted the sturdy mahogany treads, and in a poorly camouflaged attitude of defiance—a stance completely lost on Mister Harry—stepped into the shop packed with villagers.

In between covering his mouth to painfully bend over to sneeze, Mister Harry patiently took the shopping list from each curious customer, one at a time.

Her eyes, never off the shopkeeper, Ma Mabel patiently hung around till everyone had purchased their goods, packed their basket, and left. Only then did she give the sneezing man her list of groceries.

As she turned to leave, with her basket of goods balanced on the **katta** on her head, the woman who had only contempt for this brute of a man who had been nothing but a blight on Beatrice and her children, with undisguised disdain looked directly at the heavily moustached unshaven man and with more than a hint of contempt exclaimed, "Aye, Mister Harry, *yuh lucky, yuh know . . .*"

She waited for some acknowledgment from the recently

subdued man. Getting no acknowledgment, she stepped back closer to the counter, and declared, "I hear a medicine woman coming to Tapara tomorrow. So, she could check on this strange disease that every minute of the day making you sneeze."

Distressed, the shopkeeper scowled even as he buried his sore face in a little towel, and sneezed three times, grimacing painfully each time.

"A medicine woman?" the suffering man squeaked when he was able to straighten up, still keeping his eyes averted from the fearless woman.

"They call her Madam Veroux." And Ma Mabel, angrily wondering how Mister Harry ended up with what was supposed to be the dog's affliction, stared down the contemptuous man fumbling in confusion.

"Madam Veroux?" The man's jaw dropped, and his face trembled as though his heart was sinking with the news.

"But Mister Harry, how you shaking so?" Ma Mabel unsympathetically watched the once tough, rough, and indifferent Mister Harry in amazement. "You know the lady?"

Sarcasm dripped from every word.

Getting no response, she blurted out, "Aye, look how this man looking frightened!"

As usual, Mister Harry locked up the shop at five-thirty

that evening, and was hobbling to the space behind the partition, to lock away the day's earnings in the metal safe, when he jerked to a stop.

"Who is here?" he squeaked, swinging around. "Who is here?"

Someone was in the empty room with him. Though he was seeing no one he was feeling a Presence just as surely as he was feeling excruciating pain from having swung around.

HEARING VOICES

After a few weeks the blisters should have dried up, and the sneezing should have stopped.

Who was Madam Veroux? Why did he feel so terrified when Ma Mabel mentioned the name? He had never heard the name before.

Gingerly he sat on a little stool he kept back there. Why was he feeling so afraid? He knew why. He was not alone. Someone was in the shop with him. But he was not seeing anyone.

He knew he wasn't mad. Anybody could sense when another is nearby. And somebody was right there in the little room with him. Like they were watching him.

He was definitely feeling the Presence of someone. Darkness was creeping in, yet he could clearly see that the room was empty. He peered around to convince himself that he was indeed alone. Yes, he was alone.

Throwing furtive glances, the bandaged man carefully shifted his weight on the stool. With every move he endured excruciating pain. He was almost getting accustomed to the pain.

A feeling of dread akin to panic was overtaking him even as his eyes adjusted to the darkness. If there was someone in the room with him, he would see them. Why won't they show their face?

"Till the day I die", a throaty, rhythmical voice was breaking through the silence.

"You will eat . . . like a dog

And at night . . . sleep in a sty

And your memory . . . of this night

Will be gone . . . by morning light

You will wander . . . far and wide

Till scalded . . . and despised

You return here . . . to this place

Seeking out . . . her face

If she still . . . your love would be

Then from my curse . . . you will be free."

Hunched over in front his safe, Abe Chavier gazed unblinkingly out from the left side of his left eye.

Immersed in recall, he felt no pain, and although it was way past his dinner time, he also felt no hunger. As a matter of fact, time seemed to have taken his conscious awareness with it as seconds moved relentlessly into minutes, and minutes into hours.

With no awareness, there was no shop, no safe, no darkness, no body. No thought.

Then, through the silence, an awakening memory—a dull, shadowy, hazy memory—was breaking through.

Once upon a time he had been a handsome, happy young man. Things changed when that foreign woman showed up in his village. She was more than twice his age, but said she loved him. And despite his displayed disinterest in her, she stubbornly vowed that she would be his wife.

Hazy at first, but getting clearer by the moment, the picture was fleshing itself out. Feeling completely out of his league with this older woman he had become afraid of her. Afraid of, and disgusted with, her.

He had loved a beautiful teenager in the village, and had planned to make this girl his wife. When the woman one day fawned over him in a public place, he coldly but civilly told her he could never marry her because she was old enough to be his mother.

That was the first and only time he had ever spoken to her. And he hoped above hope that the woman would stop showing interest in him.

The past was coming back.

Light was breaking through the darkness of his mind. He was hearing the smooth voice of that colorful woman with demonic eyes.

She was standing over his bed.

How she had gained entrance to his room, he didn't know. He had locked his door and was lying on his bed thinking of the girl he loved when in the yellowish diffuse light of the dimmed kerosene lamp, he became aware of this attractively attired older woman standing next to his bed.

In a flash her soul-less demonic eyes pierced through his frightened eyes and dealt a vicious blow to his willpower.

Vainly struggling to stand, he felt her dusting away his resolve to stay in control of his mind.

"Till the day I die", she declared with finality, staring right through him and melting his hope to ever escape her unwelcomed attention, "you will eat like a dog, and at night sleep in a sty. . ."

In remembering, Abe Chavier felt a rising anger. He remembered how back there he struggled to hold on to his sense of personhood--to stay in control of his mind. He was reliving that moment when hope just melted away. It was like trying to stay afloat, on a moonless night, in an ocean of billowing darkness.

A GREATER POWER

So engrossed was Mister Harry in his awakening awareness, so immersed in his aroused sense of personal power, he was unaware that hours had passed since he had hobbled to the little room. Many hours.

The village had been dark for several hours, and Mister Harry was still in his shop. Word had gotten around.

Villagers, already curious about the man, for months walking around bandaged from head to foot, had heard about voices coming from the shop.

From near and far, throughout the night, young and old, husbands and wives, got out of their bed, covered themselves with protection from the dew and with quick steps made their way to Cyril Hill.

Pa Fred felt puzzled and confused. He did not know what to do with his initial suspicions about the man.

No villager had ever seen or heard Mister Harry after sunset. Not even Ma Beatrice, who had long been regretting that she had married the weird man.

Driving up Cemetery Road in Natty's jitney, Pa Fred was on his way to collect Warren's widow and their sons. Something unusual was happening. She needed to witness it for herself.

◆ ◆ ◆

The elderly man knew something Beatrice did not know for sure. Mister Harry had not gone back to the priest's house with his birth certificate, which the priest needed in order to conduct the marriage ceremony. He therefore was not really married to Beatrice.

Pa Fred, his wife, and Ma Mabel, were privy to this information. But they had all agreed to *let sleeping dogs lie*. Any disclosure would come only if the time was ever right.

None of them even knew if the priest who had agreed to conduct the strange ceremony was dead or alive. It had been more than two years. Only he would have had a copy of the marriage license if he had received Mister Harry's birth certificate.

A very capable seamstress, Beatrice on her wedding day, had looked so beautiful in her well-fitting white lace dress, and gold jewelry that she had smiled satisfyingly at her reflection in Ma Mabel's looking glass, hoping that with one glance at her, Mister Harry would find her irresistible.

Neighbors on the slope that morning had looked on happily as Pa Fred, in a black suit, turquoise shirt, black waistcoat, black bowtie, and silver chain from his pocket-watch tucked into a button hole on his jacket, had swankily swaggered down the hill, grey Wilson hat in hand.

Next to Beatrice, Ma Mabel, in an attractive pink embroidered anglaise dress, and hair stylishly stuffed into a hairnet and draped with a black lacy mantilla veil, had looked like the matronly older sister.

The three of them, Pa Fred, Ma Mabel, and Beatrice had looked very special as the photographer, hired from a distant town, focused on them signing the marriage documents. These were pictures the charming bride would treasure for life. It was just such a pity that the groom had not returned from collecting his birth certificate in time to get his picture taken, before the photographer had to pack up and leave with his bulky equipment.

Feelings of dread had been dissipating as alone in the dark room, he confronted himself.

"Who am I?" the man whispered. "Who am I?" Whispering no more, he deliberately stood.

"If she still your love would be, then from my curse you will be free."

The voice was not in the room, he slowly realized. It was in his head. As was the laughter. Laughter of power, and fate, had sealed his doom. Demonic laughter, no doubt at his cowardly fearfulness, hence his fate.

Echoes of that cackling laughter reverberated through his reverie. . . It was happening again. He was not only hearing her but also clearly seeing the elegantly fitting blouse held close at the evil woman's waistline; and the gathered skirt falling free from her hips into a flouncy flow of diabolic colorful patterns.

Dread, like smothering storm clouds was pressing down on him, pushing him into a dark abyss.

In the here and now, he once again felt strength dissipating. Hopelessness was again pinning him down, mocking his resolve to stay in control.

Again. But he wasn't yielding.

And he wasn't fighting.

Instead, consciously, Abe stood back from himself, watched the buckling feeling where new found courage was melting, and with a lift of his chin, proclaimed, "I am omnipotence! I and the Father are One!"

He had no recall of that next morning light. How did he get to this place? Familiar pictures, long hidden from memory, were surfacing.

The girl in the neighborhood. She was attracted to him. He had already saved enough money to extend the two-bedroom house he called home. He had to prepare a home for her before he asked her parents' permission to walk her up the aisle.

She knew he loved her. They had not spoken to each other about love but they both knew they loved each other. Her parents were his friends. They expected him to be their son-in-law someday.

But this foreign woman with a foreign accent settled in the village and settled her mind on him—Abe Chavier.

Who was Mister Harry? Why was he called Mister Harry?

He had since been to many different places—many, many different places—far and wide! Night time was always different from day time.

Exactly how he spent his nights he could never recall. How he managed from day to day, he did not know.

What had happened to him? And why?

Aware that he was in Tapara, he strained to remember how he ended up there. What kept coming back to him were the eyes of the foreign woman when he told her he could not be her husband because she was old enough to be his mother.

Those eyes had flashed fire--fury!

In reverie still, Abe sighed. Oblivious to the darkness in the room, he fleetingly felt his whole body raw with pain. But his attention switched right back to recall.

From sheer habit, he put away the day's earnings, and locked the safe—just as he had done every other day.

Every transaction was recorded in the blue copybook he

kept in the safe.

How he had gained access to that place, he did not know.

Now, however, vague recalls of Mister Harry were edging the strong recall of life in the town of Gleam.

He hung the key for the safe on the nail hook on the wall.

MEMORY RETURNING

On that fateful night, he had been lying on his bed thinking about his dilemma, about this woman who would not leave him alone, who kept turning up wherever he was, always speaking boldly about her love for him.

He did not tell her about Lucinda because what he had with Lucinda was none of her business.

Except for the low double bed, a wardrobe, and a small varnished brown table, his sparsely furnished room was bare.

The wardrobe. What happened to it? The money for Lucinda's engagement ring was in it—in an envelope with "Money for Lucinda's engagement ring" written on the outside.

The plans for the house were also in the wardrobe.

All his savings was in an envelope in the bottom drawer.

In remembering, Abe wondered how long he had been away from Gleam. It had to be a long time. What became of his house? Did the girl forget about him?

He sighed. Did she marry someone else? Maybe she did.

She seemed to have been convinced that he was seeing the older woman. He sighed again.

Memory, suppressed for so long, was resurfacing.

He was recalling how terrified he had been of the witch and how determined he had been to keep the girl and her family safe.

That night he had latched the door to his room, put on the padlock and locked it; and then he had gone to lie down and think.

Confused, as he watched the woman standing beside his bed, he had silently, desperately questioned himself—did I lock that door, or did I just think about locking it but forgot?

Was the house still there, he wondered. He would have to find a place to live. But first, he had to find Lucinda. He must let her know that he had not abandoned her. He had to find her, even if she was married. He had to make her understand. He had to apologize to her parents. And even if she was married, he had to tell her to her face, and in the presence of her husband that he still loved her.

He might have to start over. How old was he now? He had no idea. All his legal papers were in that wardrobe.

But would she still be interested in him?

LOVE HOLDING ON

In Gleam, Lucinda sat on Abe's sturdy double bed, looking over letters she had been receiving from church members in the towns and villages throughout the country.

Her position as a church administrator, facilitated her lifelong search for information about the man she had known she would marry someday.

As was her custom, she pressed her knees into the crocus bag rug in front Abe's bed. There she drew on her strength to continue her search for her Love.

Until she found out what had happened to him she would continue visiting his room and maintaining everything just as it was when he disappeared.

With her parents' support, she had been sending enquiries to members of her church in the towns and villages of the country. She also had a core of believers praying at the same time every week for word about him.

Since his disappearance, a bank had been established in the town of Gleam. After five years had elapsed, she had deposited his money on a joint account with her name and his. At the end of the second five years, she had hired a contractor to build the extension according to the draughtsman's plan she had found in the wardrobe.

Her father, Ron Holder, kept Abe's bike in shape. Every week he rode it for short distances in the young man's neighborhood.

In her heart, the still vivacious woman, knew that her beloved was alive. And despite what people were saying, she refused to believe that he had voluntarily abandoned her. Besides, her parents had heard about Madam Veroux and about Abe's efforts to avoid the woman.

Lucinda herself had once come face to face with the sorceress. By that time, everyone in Gleam had known who Madam Veroux was. And it had been common talk that the Madam had mashed up Lucinda's and Abe's relationship.

Abe's beloved had just stepped out of the shop in the heart of the small town when she came face to face with the colorful woman. The Madam had paused, locked her eyes onto Lucinda's, and pulling her sagging shoulders up, threw back her proud head and was opening her mouth to speak, when she looked again and felt confused under the younger woman's piercing eyes.

Fearlessness and calm funneled through a quiet anger had focused Lucinda's fixed gaze onto the middle of the woman's brow, in the location of the third eye.

Madam Veroux, confronted with the indefatigable resilience of Abe's young Love, averted her eyes, sagged her proud shoulders and hurried away from the young woman's intimidating presence.

Until they got word of Abe, Lucinda and her parents would maintain unblinking surveillance of Madam Veroux.

ECSTATICALLY HOPEFUL

Word reached Lucinda and her by then aging parents that the sorceress was due in the village of Tapara.

Tapara? The name rang a bell, and sent the church administrator sprinting off to her stack of letters.

Sure enough, there was a letter in her stack from a member in Tapara. She had received it about two years earlier. But Sister Rufina Millster had convinced her that the shopkeeper who had a vague likeness to the man Lucinda described, could not possibly be Abe Chavier.

Tapara was a half-day trip away from Gleam. It was a hilly remote village, miles off the regular public transportation route.

Lucinda owned a four-wheel drive. Her parents would accompany her, and her father, by then in his early sixties, would drive.

Beneath her calm demeanor she felt hopeful, ecstatically hopeful, intuitively aware that she was in the midst of a life-long prayer being answered one way or the other.

VIGIL ON CYRIL HILL

Outside on the steep slope of the rocky yard, the people had held an all-night vigil. So many villagers were standing or sitting on the well-swept slope, the scenario looked like a campout.

Here and there on the sides of the large yard, some had set up groupings of three rocks to make fire sides. Already some mothers had pots on the outside fires.

Meals would be prepared while the people waited to find out what was going on inside the shop.

Led by Pa Fred, Ma Beatrice and her sons had gone to their house, back of the shop, before joining the crowd on the slope. They had reported to neighbors that since the incident at the old house, no one in the family had seen or heard the dog.

With no information about the whereabouts or condition of the creature, Beatrice had chosen to stay away from Cyril Hill. They won't return till they knew for sure that the harassment was over.

A MYSTICAL DISPLAY

Madam Veroux was hissing in her heavy accent, "You fool! *Nobody rejects me and gets to boast about it!*

"Till the day I die, you will eat like a dog, and at night, sleep in a sty! And your memory of this night will be gone by morning light. You will wander far and wide, till scalded and despised you return here to this place, seeking out her face. If, she still your love would be, then, from my curse you will be free".

Abe, his head lowered, and eyes gazing straight ahead, in the darkness listened intently—not to the sorceress, but to a subtler voice.

"Who am I?" he whispered audibly. "Who am I?" he whispered louder yet.

"Who am I?" Now he was not whispering at all!

Beyond the walls, the people perked up. Silently, questioning eyes glanced at one another.

Like a helpless wreck back there, he had cringed in terror from words too damning for him to bear. He was beginning to understand what had happened to him--how he had succumbed to cheap mental trickery.

Intuitively, he knew he should have stood up to the woman, fear or no fear, and declare to her that God alone is power, and that where he is, God is. Then he should have ordered her out of his house and shut his door. He should have given her no indication that anything she said or did mattered to him.

And in the community, he should have ignored her and spent time in meditation and prayer. He should have had the whole church praying with him.

In retrospect it all seemed so clear. He had been such a fearful coward! He almost felt ashamed of himself.

Feeling a rush of righteous indignation, as he considered how this woman had diabolically mashed up his life, Abe stood to his full five foot ten inches' height, and was about to trumpet some contemptuous excoriating words against the she-devil, when he paused.

Reality was in his head. The woman wasn't even around. She bore no responsibility for what had happened to him. He had let his guard down.

She worked on the dark side of spiritual power, but he, in assuming a show of weakness, gave her permission to take control of his mind and distort his reality.

Quietly and self-confidently, the blistered and bandaged man lifted his head and affirmed, "I am my own man! I alone manage my life! I know who I am! I am strength! I am strength!"

Like every other person around her, Lucinda had been intensely leaning her ears towards the subdued voice either in monologue or dialogue, coming out of the small wooden structure a few feet ahead.

"What is he saying", Lucinda wondered. "And what does all this have to do with Abe?"

Halfway up the slope, the woman leaning on her stick as though catching her breath before resuming her climb, grunted angrily. Some eyes glanced her way, but for the most part, her grunt was lost in the darkness.

"My mind is mine! My will is mine! This universe is my home. This universe is my body! I AM in control here. Only Omnipotence has dominion over me. I AM the Eternal All in All. I alone am in charge of my destiny!"

A very puzzled expression played across Lucinda's face. Pa Fred cautiously glanced at her and at her parents. Her parents showed no sign of recognizing the voice; but Lucinda was obviously in doubt.

The voice paused. Madam, by this time, resting higher up the slope, and seemingly in a world of her own, twisted and wrangled, grunted and groaned, like one fighting some inner force, even as she leaned heavily on the stick which she gripped with both hands.

Meanwhile Lucinda, under the watchful gaze of both parents, was busy brushing away rivers of tears cascading down her cheeks.

At the same time Pa Fred's eyebrows were raising, and his eyes were widening with every new disclosure heard from the voice in the shop.

Suddenly, the voice sounded so close and loud in the darkness outside the closed wooden double doors, all perked up.

"I am my own power!"

Slowly, apprehensively, those who had been sitting, stood, and instinctively took a step backwards, as alarmed eyes, in the hazy glow of flaming flambeaux and crackling firesides, swept across the front of the shop.

"I am my own Power!" the rich bold tone ruffled the early morning stillness.

Shocked villagers turned questioning eyes on one another.

Who was behind those doors? That was not the bark of the crude Mister Harry!

Eyes slowly swung around, under twinkling stars and a waxing crescent moon, to gaze on the shaded form of an elderly woman leaning her weight, with every laborious step, onto her elegant walking stick, as she confidently picked her way to the front of the crowd.

"I am Madam Veroux, my dear friend", her musical voice rang out in response to the eloquent voice coming from the shop. "I have power over you! I manage your power!"

Their worst fears confirmed, Ron Holder, and his distraught wife, shaking with mixed emotions, supported the sagging body of their overwhelmed daughter.

All doubts cleared away, the family of three clustered with Pa Fred and his wife on the edge of the crowd just feet away from Beatrice's shop, could hardly wait to get to Abe. But something unusual was happening.

Pa Fred and his wife did not understand what was happening inside the shop. Like every other villager, they knew the voice they had been hearing was not Mister Harry's. They did not know the whole story but they had heard enough to understand what had driven the Holder family to Cyril Hill close to midnight that night. And for the visitors' sake they hoped the man they knew as Mister Harry was the person who had gone missing two decades earlier.

Without disclosing what they knew about the man, the tailor and his wife, who had met Lucinda and her parents a couple hours before cockcrow, had invited the anxious little group to join the curious morning crowd.

Hours of slow driving through the sprawling forested, hilly village, in search of the shop, had led the Holder family to villagers who had directed them to Cyril Hill.

Apprehension about finding themselves, late at night, in a strange mountain neighborhood, dissipated as in the darkness, they turned off the deserted bushy Cemetery Road into what appeared to be a crowded but quiet hillside community meeting. The silence was astounding, at first.

Flabbergasted to find themselves serendipitously in the midst of a gathering, they had discreetly enquired about who they could talk to about locating an old friend who just might be residing in Tapara under a different name.

From inside the shop, Abe's voice thundered, "I AM MY OWN POWER! I CONTROL MY OWN MIND! I ALONE AM IN CHARGE OF ME!"

Supported by both parents, drying their tears on their sleeves, Lucinda allowed rivers of tears, damned up for too long, to wash down her cheeks. And deep in the silence of her soul she cried out, "Oh God, you never fail us! You never fail us! Oh Power of love, thanks, thanks! How can I say thanks for at last guiding me to Abe!" And the woman, hidden away on the sidelines of the crowd, sat on the ground, bent over, quietly crying out, "O God, thanks! Thanks, Oh God. Oh my darling Abe, I am here with you, my Love. Right here!"

A new moon had passed the night before. There was hope in this waxing crescent phase. In less than an hour, a new day, already creeping in, would dawn.

Accepting the help of her parents to get back on her feet, she achingly willed the shut double doors of the shop to swing open.

With the power and eloquence of the apostle Paul on Mars

Hill in Athens, the spirit-driven voice rang out, "In Almighty God is my strength. In God alone is my Power!"

And as though to embrace a new awakening, the bandaged unshaven man unlatched, and threw open wide the double doors of Beatrice's shop.

Lucinda and her parents, keenly watched by Ma Rufina Millster, like every other person on the hill, gasped at the bandaged spectacle framing the doorway of the shop.

"O God Almighty!" Lucinda's legs momentarily wobbled as her heart broke and shuddered in dismay at the bandaged spectacle, and the unsightly facial hair. "What has this witch done to Abe!"

Quickly pulling herself together, she was about to dash to Abe's side when with a gentle blocking hand and fingers on his lips, Pa Fred cautioned her to wait.

Now Ma Rufina knew for sure that Mister Harry had to be Abe Chavier.

Lifting his head, in the dissolving darkness before dawn, and still locked in beyond the mundane, in that heavenly space, Abe, his tissues throbbing with divine energy, joyously affirmed, "God is in the midst of me!"

Speechless, and themselves locked into the living, throbbing energy pervading the environment, the people gazed as painlessly, the man, who just the day before could hardly make a move without wincing, and whose movements had been heavily punctuated with sneezes, effortlessly lifted his arms, and like a man of God, declared, "Father, You dwell in me, and I in you! You are the only power. In you I live and move and have my existence! God alone is. God is only good!"

Madam Veroux groaned demoniacally, and a tremor shook her body. The people next to her stumbled back.

"In Almighty Eternal I live", Abe continued, "and move, and have my Being! This body is MINE to use! Mine to manage. I am spirit. I am life. (Pause). They do not know nor do they understand; they walk about in darkness; all the foundations of the earth are shaken . . ."

The woman growled, and snarled as with both hands she gripped her sturdy walking stick trying to quiet the tremors rocking her body and to stifle the snarls, yelps, whining, and growls escaping her tight lips.

The dark night had passed; daylight was creeping in. Forms and colors were showing up in sharp contrast, but all eyes crowded around the spectacular scene unfolding in the doorway of the shop.

"All of you are gods! (Pause) All who want to live like mere men will die like mere men. (Pause) But I live and move in God! (Pause) I am God consciousness! (Pause) God is my Source! (Pause) God has brought me here! My life is hidden in God! I am spirit! (Pause) I am Truth! (Pause) I am the light. (Pause) I am light!"

Enraptured, Abe stood transfixed in the Silence as the last shades of night peeled away and the cool early morning rays of sun bathed the uplifted face in what seemed to the people, to be soft dazzling light even as Abe felt himself beholding, in heavenly rapture, a vast field of soft, translucent orange light.

Evidently immersed in a powerful transcendental state, Lucinda's long-lost Love seemed swept up and enfolded in a blissfulness that held him, though in the midst of the people, in an impenetrable silence. A palpable silence. *The Lord is in his holy temple* kind of silence. *And I, if I be lifted up will draw all men on to me* kind of silence.

Transfixed, the people, in reverential awe, gazed at Mister Harry, who, in his holy space, in that transcendent state, and with his body enshrouded in pulsating, subtle sheaths of light, was still oblivious to their presence.

"I AM LIGHT!" Soul freedom powered his clear, heavenly voice, and subtle streams of light, detected by those who had eyes to see, glowed off his extended fingertips.Then, beholden only by him, an intense glow of startling white light, intense white light, exploded in his field of vision, further locking his being down in humbling silence. Before he could gasp at the glorious mystery of the white light manifestation, in the twinkling of a moment, it was gone.

In the crowd, different people reported seeing light manifestations swirling around Mister Harry. A few described seeing a dazzle of violet rays, softening and coalescing into a pulsating halo.

For a long moment the blinding, dazzling sun rays blocked a clear view of the bandaged man as his entire body seemed to glow in a dazzling display of myriads of iridescent points of light.

For the second time this morning a collective gasp rose above the crowd. Everyone fortunate enough to be a witness to the supernatural visual display of lights astonishingly watched as all light manifestations withdrew and diffused into the atmosphere, leaving a transformed, super-refined version of a glowingly handsome, good looking, groomed Mister Harry.

Eclosion from stifling cocoon of illusion!

Freedom!

Like a messenger of God, still deep in the transformation process, Abe, with upraised arms, and still locked in the Silence, stood in the doorway of the shop.

Gushes of tears were washing down many cheeks. To a humbled, eternally grateful Lucinda, this was her long lost Love, cleansed and transformed, returned to her with Divine approval.

No trace of scalded and bandaged Mister Harry. Not a lingering trace!

Silence reigned on the slope. Silence prevailed. Profound silence. Awesome silence. A "*God is in this place*" kind of silence. "*Let all the earth be silent*" kind of silence.

And Abe Chavier, immersed in this silence, remained transfixed, with eyes closed and arms tirelessly uplifted. He and God alone in that transcendental state, in that holy space.

After what seemed to be an eternity of awesome silence,

Pa Fred nudged Lucinda, indicating she could go and claim her gentleman.

As the stately woman with a soft gaze made her way to the shop's entrance, to the man caught up in a trance-like state, Madam Veroux, obviously stunned by the appearance of the younger woman, glowered at her, and maliciously swung out her walking stick.

Lucinda paused and quietly turned her gaze on the location of the woman's third eye.

Reluctantly, the aged sorceress shrunk back, withdrew her stick, and averted her gaze.

Without opening his eyes, Abe knew this was Lucinda standing at his side. Too much time had passed since they had been together. How much time, he did not know.

Love's electricity tingled his heart, and he did something he had not done for a long while. He smiled—a sparkling, radiating, mind-body-and soul, joyful smile.

Only the Supreme Eternal could have brought them together like this.

Whatever had kept them apart was now dissolved—completely dissolved. With face still uplifted, and eyes still closed, Abe slipped his strong, reenergized arm around the waist of his beloved, even as her tear-beclouded gaze embraced and bathed his renewed countenance.

A long thoughtful gaze followed the opening of his clear

sparkling eyes. It was as though overnight the love of his life had morphed from the young coy teenager into this serene, composed, statuesque beauty before him. Resisting the urge to sweep her into his arms, he, with patient restraint, passionately smiled on her. And she, slipping her arm around his waist, with less restraint, held him tight, and through tumbling tears, smiled back.

They looked perfectly matched and unabashedly in love.

MA MABEL

Ma Mabel did not know if to laugh or cry. She did not know if to kneel or dance. She wondered if what she had witnessed the day before was a dream or reality.

Madam Veroux had just finished telling her about the young man she had cursed, when Robert arrived with a message from Pa Fred saying she needed to come to the shop right away.

The time was about five in the morning.

As was her custom, Ma Mabel had been out of bed around three thirty and had already prepared breakfast. The sorceress had arrived the night before and had stayed in an extra room at Ma Mabel's home.

According to Madam Veroux, there were only two ways the curse could be lifted from the young man—either with her death or with the young lady's acceptance of the man just as he was.

By this time Ma Mabel had been pretty sure that Mister Harry was the cursed man, but she kept this to herself. Subsequent events suggest that somehow Madam Veroux was aware that she was on the trail of Abe Chavier, the man who had eluded her since that night in his room.

Ma Mabel did venture to ask Madam Veroux what if the man with the curse had been hurt or disfigured while under the curse, would he still be that way when the curse was lifted—whether it was lifted by the sorceress' death or by the acceptance of the man's former Love.

Madam Veroux was emphatic when she proclaimed that the man would be restored to his youthful vigor and beauty when the curse was broken.

However, the sorceress declared, whereas Abe Chavier's former Love would have aged to look twice as old as she was when Abe knew her, Abe would not have aged at all. His former love would therefore look almost twice as old as he. Further, memory of himself under the curse would be erased, while memory of his life before the curse would be restored.

Of all Madam Veroux's pronouncements about Abe Chavier only one proved to be partially correct—the restored Abe Chavier recognized no one in Tapara. Immediately however, he recognized the presence of Lucinda's parents, though they both had aged considerably. Madam Veroux, he did not recognize at all.

He did however, marvel at the older woman's audaciousness when she edged up close to him and whispered, "Abe darling, don't you remember me?"

"No ma'am, I don't", he quipped as keenly he observed Lucinda's aversive response to the woman. Putting an arm around his beloved's shoulder, he gazed compassionately on her and stepped away from the woman.

"I am Madam Veroux", the woman chirped, as Abe, holding Lucinda close to his side, walked away.

"Sorry Granny", he paused, and looked kindly at the woman, "I don't think I am acquainted with your name". And Abe went with his Love, past gawking eyes, to join her parents.

But something else had been happening at the foot of the hill. A strange van had driven into the big yard and parked.

"Daddy! Daddy! Daddy!"

Dumbfounded, the entire hillside had been further silenced by Calvin's and Joshua's delirious shrieks as the boys ran into the open arms of their Uncle Waldo, before fearfully backing away, looking terrified and confused.

Canaan and Elijah had silently stared, puzzled by their brothers' strange behavior.

The people's attention had been torn between what was happening between Abe and Lucinda, and what was happening at the foot of the hill. But they had stayed riveted on Abe.

Ma Mabel, recalling the events, smiled to herself.

Telbut's mother had reverently walked up to the man she had watched with her own eyes, emerge from a glowing nest of dazzling light rays. Timorously, she had asked, how could he not recognize Beatrice and her children.

Still protectively holding Lucinda close to his side, the newly transformed man had courteously and empathically explained that he was trying to make sense of what was happening to him. The last time he had seen his love, she was a teenager; but there in his arms, she was a beautiful matured adult.

He had to get her help to understand what happened to the years in between. The only reality he was aware of was of himself as Abe Chavier.

By this time, Waldo Bartelay, the "spitting image" of Warren Bartelay, was slowly walking up the hill even as he paused to look at his nephews and the beloved wife of his late brother.

Gasps of momentary confusion accompanied every glance of recognition directed at him, even as all ears stayed glued to conversations around Abe.

Ahead of Waldo, at the top of the slope, in the midst of buzzing excitement, Abe had asked about the identity of Beatrice and her children, and tightening his grip on Lucinda, had expressed alarm that somewhere in those lost years he had married and had children. Was he suffering from amnesia, he wondered aloud.

With mighty relief the transformed man and the woman who had spent her youth searching for him heard that neither of them had any need to be concerned. Even in that other life from which he had just been delivered, he had been a strange man, with no interest in amorous relationships. And actually, unknown to many, he had not even signed documents for the marriage he had neither arranged nor cared about.

Pa Fred gazed lovingly at the young man, even as Waldo became aware that the people's attention was riveted on the glowing features of a handsome young man and his stately, lovely female companion.

Abe did not know why Pa Fred seemed so excited while talking with him. But he was coming to accept that he was out of touch with a large chunk of his memory. He trusted Lucinda to explain to him later why he was in that strange place in the midst of a crowd of people early in the morning. And why he seemed to be the center of focus.

"My boy, Abe", and ole Pa Fred chuckled.

From outside the circle, a very happy Waldo, excited to be at last in Tapara, looked on.

"Abe, oh Abe", Pa Fred chimed, chuckling still. "Somebody had put you under a curse and thought they alone had power to break that curse, but young man, you are God's messenger to all of us here in Tapara".

So that was it—he had been under a curse! Apparently, for a long time. The elderly man was the first person to offer an explanation to what was happening.

And Waldo, a new arrival on the hill about to become a new member of the community, had been getting an unbelievable introduction to a story he might never fully comprehend.

Pa Fred, Ma Mabel smiled, could have hardly contained the pride and joy oozing from his demeanor as he addressed Abe. "You have shown us that you had the power in you to escape that curse. Son, you had that power all along.

"Despite all you had gone through, and God in heaven knows you went through dark nights, you stayed true to yourself, and true to your lovely Lucinda. You are a pure soul, Abe. I have known you for a few years well.

"Well", Pa Fred had checked himself, "Not you, not you at all, but the personality the curse had you hiding in. I was around that personality. And even in that personality you stayed true to yourself.

"It took all that time for you to discover that you have the power to take care of your mind and your body—years to discover that nobody could control your mind if you don't give in to them. Abe, my boy, you have always been a free man. You just had to claim that freedom."

Of course, Abe could not appreciate Pa Fred's enthusiasm. He was a stranger in a strange place. And the information he was getting was stranger still.

"Abe Chavier was never lost; just misplaced in the identity of Mister Harry. You took years to discover that you alone have been responsible for everything you went through, because when you were ready to escape the curse, you, Abe Chavier, shook yourself out of that stupor and released yourself."

Pa Fred's eyes below the graying eyebrows, twinkled. "You

freed yourself, my boy. You engineered your own escape". The village tailor and elder was still in awe of the supernatural manifestation he had moments before witnessed.

His heart throbbing with excitement, he had gripped Abe's shoulder lovingly. He wanted to embrace the young man, but Abe was not removing his arm from around the stately, beautiful Lucinda.

"What you needed you always had, Abe, my boy. But this day you discovered the Truth that only you had the power to free yourself! You discovered the truth."

With keen interest Lucinda listened to every word Pa Fred uttered. Abe did not understand, but she, after decades of not knowing what had befallen her beloved, was thankful for any information about those lost years.

"Thank you," Abe was meeting Pa Fred for the first time. These people were celebrating with him. He had to thank them.

After accepting the blessings of those who eagerly grabbed hold of his hand, he turned to the people around him. "Thanks to all of you for whatever you have done for me. And my deepest apologies for whatever offense I might have caused all of you. If you would excuse me, there is one thing I have to do right away."

Like every other person on that hill at that time that morning, Waldo pressed close to look at Abe and the lovely woman in his embrace.

Watching his every move, the people had crowded around the former Mister Harry, transfixed, even as they had positioned themselves at every vantage point to capture every move he made.

Standing off from Lucinda, Ma Mabel was recalling, Abe, basking in the warm morning sun, had faced the love of his life, she who had spent her youth searching for him--he had taken her hands into his, and intently, under many curious stares, had carefully examined her fingers.

“My love”, he had said after the visual examination, even as he affectionately looked her in the eyes, “Forgive me for asking, but I need to know . . .”

“What?” Puzzled, Lucinda, unblinkingly, watched him in the eye.

“Are you married to another?”

“Ever since you mysteriously disappeared twenty-two years ago, my Love, I have been diligently searching for you, night and day, and praying for your return. I have had no extra time or extra love to share with another man, Abe. I think if I had never found you, I would have gone to my grave searching still.”

Abe allowed himself a full minute to soak in the magnitude of Lucinda’s love for, and devotion to, him.

“Mister and Mrs. Holder”, Abe fixed his gaze on the glowing countenances of Lucinda’s parents, “do we have your blessing to be married?”

“Yes, of course”, Ron Holder and his wife spoke with one voice, as they stepped closer to the young man they always thought of as a son-in-law.

Then Ron Holder gazed into the clear eyes of the young man his daughter had spent her youth trying to locate.

"My Son, greatly beloved, we are on the Mount of Transfiguration with you". Ron Holder reached for Abe's free hand. "You can never imagine how we all have lived for this reunion, although we could have never hoped for anything as miraculous and spectacular as what we witnessed here today. Son, at one moment you were bandaged from head to toes, it seemed; then the light of glory filled this place and here you are, transformed. Not a trace of distress; not a blemish on your transformed body. And an outfit designed and delivered by the master tailor himself."

"I agree; I agree." Pa Fred took the liberty to touch the neckline of Abe's shirt, and to stand off in admiration of the delicate sheen of his pants material.

Ron Holder continued, "I will be shouting praise and thanks to the Almighty for a long while for what we have experienced here today."

Waldo was a bit startled as the crowd, behaving like a congregation, intoned, "Amen! Thanks God Almighty! Amen!"

Ron Holder continued, "Lucinda has not allowed any of us in Gleam to forget about you for the past twenty-two years. For weeks after you disappeared, we were afraid she would go mad. . .."

Eager to know about Mister Harry's past, the villagers

crowded closer to hear what Ron Holder was saying.

". . . Nobody could console her. Then one day she pulled herself together, all by herself, and went back to school. Within a few months she graduated with high honors. By then her mother and I noticed that overnight she had become a woman, with a purpose. And even as she attended to her own development, and focused on taking care of your property and your affairs she never tired of enquiring in every part of this country for word about you. She had groups in every district in this country praying for you at the same time every week. God has returned you to Lucinda."

"I am a member of the Tapara Prayer group that prays every week for any word about you". Rufina Millster had stepped close to Abe and Lucinda.

Lucinda acknowledged Kenneth's Mom.

"We meet for prayer session once a week", Sister Rufina informed a grateful and thankful Abe. "On behalf of our group, I shout thanks".

And tears tumbled down the cheeks of Rufina Millster, even as many wiped the tears from their own eyes.

"And I sing glory to the name of Jehovah for bringing both of you back together again after a lifetime of praying and waiting. This is the greatest miracle I could ever hope to see."

Abe's eyes stayed on Lucinda's face awash with tears even as he listened first to her father, and then to Rufina Millster.

"We are in Tapara for the first time, Abe", Ron Holder continued, "because Lucinda had people keeping track of the miserable woman—the sorceress who tried to destroy you because you refused to marry her."

Abe shifted his gaze from his beloved and looked at her father. "What are you talking about, Pa?"

Heads turned to watch Madam Veroux hurrying down the slope, trying to lose herself in the crowd.

Abe was still trying to absorb what he was hearing, when on impulse he let go of Lucinda's hands and slipped his hand into his pocket.

Around him, people watched his movement curiously. He took out a small box from his pocket. Lucinda, like many around, gasped.

"Pa", Abe said, "I know the Almighty is here now. Right here, right now. Do you believe as I do?"

"Yes!" the people thundered.

"Then there is no better place to do what I propose to do right now." And turning to Lucinda, Abe asked, "Love, will you marry me?"

"Yes", Lucinda, for the first time since recovering her long lost Love, wiped both hands across her tear-washed cheeks, and responded almost in a whisper.

"Right here, right now?"

"Yes, Abe, my Love. But don't we need a cleric?"

"Pa", Abe turned to Ron Holder, "Will you stand in for the cleric?"

Before Ron Holder could think of a response, Waldo Bartelay stepped up to Abe. "I am a Minister of the Gospel. Here is my license", and Waldo opened a leather wallet, took out a folded document, and showed it to Abe.

"So many questions", Abe mused as they headed for the city with his father-in-law at the steering wheel.

"I have just taken unto myself a wife, but where will I accommodate you? I don't even know what has become of my house. I had planned to extend it but I was waiting till I got your parents' permission to consult with you about the design. I will have to start over. My savings must be moth-eaten by now. But I'm not worried. Everything will work out well for us."

"Yes, my Love", Lucinda smiled, "everything is already working out well for us."

And a happy Lucinda, wearing a shiny gold wedding band on that special finger, nestled her head on her husband's chest as he wrapped his loving arms around her.

END

EPILOGUE

Hours after Abe had driven off with Lucinda and her parents, the people were still clustered in little groups on the hill. They could not stop talking about what had happened on Cyril Hill that morning.

There was still a hush over the place. A reverence that could be felt.

The people could not stop telling and retelling their stories.

Calvin and Joshua had rushed into the shop as soon as Abe had stepped away from the doorway. Calvin had quickly located the key to the safe.

With wide opened eyes, and open mouth, the boys had found their mother.

To their amazement, the safe was packed with cash. Mister Harry had not taken any of their money.

Their mother hugged them, and said, "I am not sure what is happening, Calvin, and Joshua, but I know that God is in this place."

"Mama", Calvin held his mother's hand, "I am feeling so wonderful. I know that you, Joshua, Canaan, Elijah, and I won't have anything to worry about ever again. I just want to shout".

Beatrice giggled for the first time in years.

"I feel the same way, Son", she said.

Canaan held on to his mother's other hand and did a little jump. "Mama, I feel so happy. I can't believe that such a nice man was hiding inside Mister Harry all this time", and the boy laughed happily.

Winston, Errol, Jonathan, Kenneth, Telbut, and Stefan huddled together in the crowd. They were mostly silent.

Ma Mabel walked towards them. They understood her reverent silence.

Together, they found Ma Beatrice. She was sitting on the slope outside the shop, surrounded by her children.

"How's your belly, Beatrice?" Ma Mabel sat next to the dumbfounded mother.

Beatrice gently touched her belly. Her face registered shock. She pressed her hand against the sore spot. Then she said, "Ma Mabel, here, press your hand here. Press it hard."

Canaan and Elijah jumped to their feet and watched their Mama. "Mama", Elijah watched his mother quizzically, "your belly is not hurting anymore?" And he threw up his arms and laughed.

Canaan hugged his Mama. "God healed you, Mama?" he asked. "God healed you when he was healing Mister Harry?"

"It looks so, Canaan", Beatrice laughed.

"God is in this place, Beatrice", Ma Mabel whispered. "God is in this place."

The teenagers smiled with Ma Beatrice, and they smiled with one another.

"Aye Telbut!" Nazir tapped Telbut on his shoulder. The boy was smiling excitedly. "Look!" he shouted. "Look!"

All the boys stood up and watched Nazir in amazement. The little boy twirled around. "I have two normal legs. No more one normal and one short! "And the boy couldn't stop grinning.

"And my grandpa stopped coughing. He is here in the crowd."

Winston sat down, then stood up again.

"You realize something is happening around here, *fellahs*?" Errol asked. "Winston, you must be thinking what I am thinking."

"I am going down the road to see if anything happened to my father." Winston made one step to descend the hill but in happy shock, stood still.

"You don't have to, Son. I am right here". Pa Ali was walking out of the crowd to embrace his son. "Something happened to me this morning. Praise to Allah. To God be the glory." Tears of joy were washing down Pa Ali's face.

"Telbut", Errol turned to Ma Mabel's son. "Lift up your shirt."

"Lift up my shirt? Telbut protested. "Why?"

Along with Ma Mabel, the boys all strained and stretched to get a look at Telbut's back.

"God is in this place," Kenneth said. "Abe Chavier was in front us all these years, under a curse, but when God was ready he threw back the curse and freed Abe Chavier. God answered the lady's prayers. He answered the prayers of all the groups praying for Abe. And when he was freeing Abe Chavier, he must have said, "I will just free all these people around Abe one time".

Something was exciting the crowd at the foot of the hill. Beatrice moved down the hill to see what the commotion was about. Calvin, and Joshua, screamed, "Daddy! Daddy! Daddy!"

The people pressed back towards the houses, leaving a clear path for Beatrice and the man her children were calling 'Daddy'.

Some remembered Warren's twin brother who had visited Tapara for Warren's and Beatrice's wedding. He had taken the boat back to the motherland. When he heard of Warren's sickness, he vowed never to marry anyone in the big country, but to work and save so he could return to Tapara and take care of his brother's family. He had come in a van, and had brought boxes and suitcases for Warren's family.

Pa Fred and Ma Mabel agreed that a powerful Presence had been released in Tapara that day. And it was a presence that came with the restoration of Abe Chavier.

"Where is Madam Veroux?" Ma Mabel asked. She had forgotten about the melodramatic, flamboyant seventy-something-year-old woman who dressed very stylishly. Maybe Pa Fred would know where the woman was, she thought.

As she was stepping over to Pa Fred's house, she saw an old woman she had not seen before. The woman was about one hundred years old. She was bent and wrinkled, but could walk without a stick. And she wore a long skirt, grey with age, a faded long-sleeve blouse, and a faded head wrap.

"Granny", Ma Mabel addressed the old woman, "Where is your home?"

"I don't have a home", the old woman spoke cheerily. I can take care of myself, but I need a place to stay. Any old place would do. Can you help me? I can wash and clean house. You think young Beatrice would need somebody to help her clean out and take care of her boys?"

"Madam Veroux?" Telbut's mother exclaimed, as she bent over and took a good look at the old woman's face. "You're not going back to Gleam?"

"You mistake me for somebody else" the vibrant old woman jauntily replied. "I don't know any place called, Gleam, and my name is not Madam Veroux. I am just a homeless, penniless old woman in need of some place to lay my head. Will you help me?"

END OF EPILOGUE

GLOSSARY OF TERMS

Ah ever see—I've ever seen

Allyuh—you, or you all

'Bandon—Abandoned land; bushy, unattended land in the neighborhood

Bathe off—also referred to as "sponge off"—to take a partial bath, including washing face, legs and arms

But allyuh ent notice? —Didn't you-all see? Didn't you observe?

Callaloo—a delicious Caribbean soup-like dish made from the leaves of the dasheen plant and ochro. Green in color. Often boiled in coconut milk and heavily spiced with green seasonings. Sometimes cooked with crab, pig tail, or salt beef.

Cascadura—a small catfish--a Trinidad delicacy

Cocoyea broom—broom made from the spines of coconut leaves. Used to sweep yards

Cooked up—to come up with a plan

Cut eye—Hard, harsh mean look from one side of the eye

Dat--That

Dawg—A human appearing as a dog

De man—the man

De--the

Ent—is not. Not so?

Farse—out of place; impertinent

Farseness—impertinence; way out of line

Fellah—guy, male acquaintance, pal

Figs—bananas; green figs

Fight fire with fire—to use same methods others use against you; or even to hit them harder than they hit you

Finger-lickin—very tasty

Flambeaux—home-made torches; made from a bottle like a beer bottle filled with kerosene, with a piece of rag stuck into bottle mouth to form a wick

Gallery--verandah

Gayippe—a group teaming together to get a job done. Example: Group of men working together to build another's house

Going to make—will be making

Ground provision—root crops; e.g. potatoes, cassavas, dasheen, eddoes

Have sweet hands-- Capable of cooking very delicious meals

I hear— I have heard that

Jus so—suddenly; without warning

Jinx—Bad luck; a curse

Katta—a thick coil of cloth placed on the head to cushion weight—bucket of water, basket of goods, bundle of wood, et cetera. carried on head

Left in the dark—left uninformed; not given desired information

Lorha—a cylindrical small, smooth stone used as a rolling pin by villagers;

Manicou--opossum

Monkey know what tree to climb—People know who they would risk interfering with; or taking chances with

Nah—no

Oui—French for yes, yeah

Paid no mind—give no attention to; to not bother with

Pick their mouth—try to get information from them

Pitch oil—kerosene

Pot Hound—a dog of no specific breed; a mutt or mongrel

Provision—starchy vegetables, some grown in the ground, and some, like breadfruit, green figs (bananas), and plantain, grow above ground

Salt fish—salted cod

Sill—large flat stone on which villagers ground masala, using lorha

Sim—a short, flat bean pod; delicious curried

Straining his ears—listening very intently, struggling to hear

Sweet soap---toilet soap; bath soap, such as Palmolive, Lux, and Carbolic soap.

Tattoo—armadillo; called tattoo in Trinidad and Tobago

Throw an eye—to glance quickly while paying attention

To cook up—to come up with a plan--a plot

Tom tom balls—cooked breadfruit (pembwa) pounded into a mush with mortar and pestle, then shaped into balls. Also made with cooked plantain

Torchlight--flashlight

Tuberculosis—A contagious disease that affects the lungs. Caused by a strain of bacteria

Warbine—fresh water fish; found in ravines in Trinidad

Washykong--crepe-soles, tennis shoes, sneakers

Wotless—a person of no good reputation; worthless

Yuh—you, or your

Yuh lucky, yuh know—Do you realize how lucky you are! You are really lucky

PRONUNCIATIONS

Arouca—Ah roo kuh

Bartelay—Bah tih lay

Callaloo—kah luh loo

Chavier—Sha veer

Dawg—human appearing as a dog

Flambeaux—flam bo

La Diablesse—On the island, pronounced, Lah juh bles

Ligahoos—lih guh who; also lagahoo

Lucinda—Loo sin duh

Oui--Wee

Rufina—Roo fee nuh

Soucouyants—Soo koo yahnt

Tapara—Tuh pah rah

Veroux –Vay roo

REVIEW QUESTIONS

1. How did the people of Tapara feel about young Beatrice?
2. Warren Bartelay knew he had to meet Beatrice's parents. Why?
3. List any traits Pa Alfred Worrell appreciated seeing in Warren.
4. Why did Ma Beatrice move to her old family house?
5. Name two persons in Tapara who provided needed services.
6. Why didn't Abe just ask Lucinda to marry him?
7. Compare Warren's approach to marriage with Abe Chavier's.
8. How did Warren Bartelay provide for his family, financially?
9. Name Warren's sons. How would their memories differ?
10. Young Ma Beatrice kept Ma Cyril busy. In what way?
11. Was Ma Beatrice capable of managing her business? Why?
12. What is a gayippe?
13. How did Pa Fred contribute to community building in Tapara?
14. What are some table manners Warren taught his sons?
15. Name two persons in this story you admire. Say why.
16. What are breadfruit tom tom balls?
17. What did Warren Bartelay do between dinner and bedtime?
18 How did Ma Beatrice avoid starting a forest fire?
19. Where did Mister Harry come from?
20. Did Mister Harry propose to the widow, Beatrice?
21. What did Mister Harry want from Beatrice?
22 How much is thirty-six degrees Celsius in Fahrenheit?
23. True or false. To convert Celsius to Fahrenheit, multiply Celsius temperature by 9 (nine), divide by 5 (five), and

add 32 (thirty-two).

24. How was Madam Veroux able to control Abe Chavier?

25. Try this. Think of something that happened to you a long time ago. Observe your posture as you go into deep thought. How are you holding your head? Where are your eyes focused?

26. Despite his uncouth behavior, Mister Harry was at heart a gentleman. What in this story supports this statement?

27. "Scalded and despised" Were Mister Harry's injuries the result of accident, or fate? If you think something else, what? Explain.

28. Name two women who wanted to marry Abe.

29. What synonym for graveyard is found in this story?

30. How did being proactive help Lucinda find her long lost Love?

31. What were Winston and Errol determined to find out after they saw Nazir dancing and laughing joyously?

32. How were Lucinda and her parents able to be in place to witness Abe's transcendental transformation?

33. Why was Madam Veroux yelping and snarling?

34. How did Ma Rufina's son, Kenneth, account for the multiple healings that occurred in the community that morning?

35. Try explaining the presence of Nazir and his grandfather on the slope that morning.

36. What was happening with Abe inside the shop that night? What could have happened to his memory all those years?

37. What proclamation of Abe Chavier signaled the release of Madam Veroux's hold on him?

38. Considering that Mister Harry did not recognize the name, Madam Veroux, how would you explain his fright when Ma Mabel told him Madam Veroux would visit Tapara the next day?

39. The voice Mister Harry was hearing in the back room, where do you think it was coming from? Explain.

40. Would Abe Chavier have benefitted from attempting to take revenge on Madam Veroux?

41. How were Pa Cyril Fred's organizing skills evident that morning on the hill?

42. How did hurting Abe Chavier benefit Madam Veroux?

43. Why do you think the author had all those people meeting

in front the shop that night?

44. During recall, and reverie, Mister Harry had periods of painlessness. How do your account for this?

45. "Vengeance is mine, saith the Lord, "I will repay". What in this story supports this statement? Explain.

46. Sometimes when forced to face your worst fears you could be shaken free of fear. How does this statement apply in this story?

47. While he was still in Mister Harry's body, Abe struggled with the anger he felt towards the witch. How did he use this anger to his benefit?

48. Was Abe being wise in completely ignoring Madam Veroux?

49. When would Abe have been aware that many years had elapsed since he had seen Lucinda?

50. In the final analysis was Abe Chavier a blight or a blessing to Beatrice and the people of Tapara?

51. Why did Errol tell Telbut to lift his shirt?

52. With Mister Harry out of her life, what do you think were the chances of Beatrice marrying a second time?

53. Can you repeat Abe Chavier's words as you imagine he spoke them, as he pushed open the doors of the shop that early morning?

54. Abe had to quietly accept that so much had changed since he had last seen Lucinda. He was in for lots of surprises. How many of these surprises can you name?

55. "Subdued avian melodies" To what is the author referring?

56. In olden days many families had dump heaps in their back yard, or on nearby vacant lots. What would have been some consequences of dumping bottles and cans on the premises?

57. What are tonka beans and hog plums? Which one is used as a spice?

58. Ma Mabel intervened at significant junctures in this story. Describe two of these interventions.

59. How did Lucinda's life change the first day of Abe's return?

60. Compare Mr. Harry in the back room that night with the man Lucinda reclaimed as her Love the next morning.

61. Name three different kinds of soap Ma Beatrice had to get from the shop. What was each used for?

62. Ma Rufina Millster was of great help to Lucinda. How?

63. What could have been Mister Harry's reason for wanting

    Beatrice and her children staying away from visiting the cemetery?

64. Why could Mister Harry not have been married to Ma Beatrice?

65. It is said that "what you sow, you reap". How did this saying apply to Madam Veroux?

66. Do you think Lucinda was afraid of Madam Veroux? Give reason for your answer.

67. What do you think caused Ma Beatrice's family to lose their fright of the scalded creature in their house that night?

68. Who were Calvin and Joshua excitedly calling, "Daddy"? Explain why this person was on Cyril Hill that morning.

69. Light manifestations were involved in Abe's healing. What do you know about light manifestations and the human body?

70. "Everything is already working out well for us." Who spoke these words? What surprises did this person have for Abe?

AFTERWORD

Many years ago, as a girl growing up in my homeland, Trinidad and Tobago, I listened to several stories about people magically changing their human forms at nights. Always at nights, when outside was pitch black. At that time, there were no street lights, and most of the village homes did not have electricity.

As a child I was afraid of the dark. mostly because of the scary creatures I heard adults say, moved about in the dark.

Soucouyants, la diablesse, douens, and ligahoos, were names given some of these creatures.

Most of the stories were told by one of the greatest story tellers, I had known, my paternal grandma, Julia (Ashton), a Vincentian by birth.

Grandma Julia, as a young girl of African and what then was called Carib ancestry, was sent from her home in Rose Hill, St. Vincent to stay with relatives in Trinidad. Born in the eighteen hundreds, she was an entrepreneurial person.

As a young mother, residing in Arouca, she was walking along the Lopinot Road about three o'clock one morning, on her way to the hills to collect oranges to sell. She had just entered a short tunnel (under the train tracks) when a large black hog with a band of white around its neck, wobbled past her.

Stiff with tension and fearless as a mule, she hardened her jaws and gutturally grunted, "Hmmmm!"

She hadn't gone far when around the bend, in the dim moonlight, she saw a very tall man in a black suit, and white collar approaching. "Madam" he paused as he approached her, "you see a black pig pass here?"

"Hmmmm!" from deep in her throat the intimidating grunt escaped, shaking her head with a deliberate tremor, as she with firm steps, and looking neither to the right or to the left, continued her trek up the dark valley road. Evidently the man was a ligahoo, as were the creatures my Dad had told me about.

According to my Dad, who was born in 1914 in Arouca, one dark night on his way home from visiting friends, as he reached the corner at Waterloo Road and the Eastern Main Road, a donkey playfully pranced up and down in front him. Then an adolescent, Dad snatched up a piece of wood from the grassy roadside, and landed a hard blow on the animal's back.

Early next morning a gentleman was in front his mother's door. He asked that she tell her boy when he sees anything in the night, not to interfere with it.

Another night, a moonlight night, Dad said, he was again walking along Waterloo Road, passing the cemetery, when he saw a fowl walking among the graves. Picking up a stone, he pelted the fowl. The bird, he reported, cackled, and flew straight up in the air. Straight up. I never figured out how to classify that fowl. A ligahoo? I don't know.

Occasionally I heard stories about an old woman here or there shedding her skin at night, transforming herself into a ball of fire, and sailing across to her victim's house, where as a ball of fire she would enter under the eaves of the roof, and suck the sleeping female victim. Some women swore that if they awoke with blue black marks on their thigh, or on any other part of their body, a soucouyant had sucked them.

Then there was the la diablesse. One story I heard was about a charming young man, who was walking along the Eastern Main Road, through the "high woods", now known as the Cleaver Woods of D'Abadie". Well dressed, he was returning from a function in Arima when he saw a beautiful young woman in a long flowing skirt, walking ahead of him. He quickly caught up with her, and turned on his charms. Together, they left the road, and walked into the woods. She laughed loud and mockingly as she turned away from the "picka" patch (patch of thorny bush) into which she had left him, trapped. If he hadn't been so terrified he would have noticed that she had one human foot, and one bovine hoof.

The concept which has developed and blossomed into "Abe & Lucinda/The Curse" challenged my creativity back there in the late nineteen seventies while I was a permanent resident in the USA. A friend at The Smithsonian Institution of Washington, D.C., had suggested that I write a folk tale. Not knowing where to start I tossed around ideas in my mind till a thought sprouted some roots. In 2015 I pursued a story line and published a version under the title, "What's Up With That Dawg?". I next published "Mister Harry", another version. Not satisfied with that publication, or with the cover, I published yet another version, "The Curse".

Here in 2019 I am finally satisfied with how I have presented and resolved the problem encapsulated in the folktale, "Abe & Lucinda/The Curse".

Thanks to Dr. Roy Bryce-LaPorte (originally from Panama) who then headed African and Caribbean studies at The Smithsonian Institution, for encouraging me back there to write a folk tale.

Settling down to produce this contribution to Trinidad and Tobago literature, I naturally thought of the folk stories my paternal grandma and my Dad had told us—stories about l*igahoos, la diablesse,* and *soucouyants*.

Eugenia Springer, February 12, 2019
D'Abadie, Trinidad, T&T

BOOKS BY THIS AUTHOR

Words Of A Caribbean Woman (Eugenia's Poetry)

POETRY FROM THE SOUL

Celebratively, the soul of this all-embracing Caribbean woman captures in poetry, the longings, aspirations, and dreams of life.

Family Relationships/Dear Dr. Springer

ANSWERS TO QUESTIONS ON RELATIONSHIPS

Family Life Consultant responds to questions about love, trust, marriage, parenting, self-esteem, reproductive issues, gender and sexuality, crime, and more.

Korruptors/Wrong&Strong

A NOVEL--FICTION
Story unfolds in the country of TRINILAND

Julia Gordio, a powerful cartel madam, hires an indebted business partner to retrieve a lucrative government contract, fraudulently and nepotically awarded to a small businessman. The reluctant, unwilling conscripted man brings along an unsuspecting blokish partner. Mission accomplished, the madam sets out to eliminate witnesses. Going after the bloke could be her undoing.

The Spiritual Journey/Gethsemane & The Wilderness

FROM A LIFE OF UNCERTAINTY TO KNOWING SELF

The author shares her story of being guided from a life of uncertainty and insecurity to an understanding of her true identity. Not at all an easy road but immensely self-fulfilling and satisfying.

Tantie Pearlie's Funeral

THE VILLAGE FUNERAL--CELEBRATION OF LIFE

The author uses the fictitious character, Tantie Pearlie, to depict village life in the neighborhood in Trinidad that cradled her development in early life.

Communication For Survival/It Didn't Have To End So

COMMUNICATION SKILLS FOR HEALTHY RELATIONSHIPS

"Communication for Survival/It Didn't Have to End So" The stories in this publication, dedicated to all peoples of my homeland, Trinidad and Tobago, are written to illustrate how changing our style of communication can modify the outcome of our interactions. Each story is written in two versions. The first version, illustrates the kinds of tragic outcomes that can be triggered off when we are not feeling balanced within ourselves, and the second version--Ending Differently--illustrates the more desirable outcomes that could result when we feel more balanced within ourselves.

Girl And Her Therapist

WORKING WITH A VICTIM OF INCEST -- PSYCHODRAMA

In Part One of this volume, "Girl and Her Therapist", the author uses psychodrama to present the nightmarish horror of the person violated. Rather than abandon the violated to despair, the author arouses in the character a realization of her innate power to confront the problem and bring it to a resolution. In the second part of this volume, the author reaches out to all bogged down in guilt and shame and points out the path to freedom. Within the covers of this book is a challenge to any laboring under the pain of self-loathing, hate, and shame, to release the hate, and shame and reclaim their power to make of their life what they will. And this challenge is also extended to any now bogged down with guilt and remorse for having in the past been a perpetrator/abuser.

Words Of Wisdom/Further Insights Into The Journey

Author's Journey From FEARFULNESS TO RELATIVE FEARLESSNESS

Through prose and poetry the author shares from deep within, her slow, gradual evolution from fear-based living--So cramped by my lack of initiative; Wanting, but afraid to pursue; Having/ but only in imagination . . . to increasing self-confidence--We find ourselves doing the things we always wanted to do. And we know now there is no chance of failure. . . . It is unbelievably wonderful at this stage of the journey, looking out at life from this place of inner strength, this place of centeredness, this place of heaven within.

Limited number of copies. journeybooks43@gmail.com

Abe & Lucinda/The Curse

A FOLKTALE

Awakened from twenty-years of amnesia, he remembers the girl he had been intent on marrying, before the sorceress disrupted his life.

Made in the USA
Columbia, SC
21 November 2023